Ridicule

A NOVEL BY

ALTHEA JEWEL

Printed in the United States of America
First Edition, December 2023

ISBN Number 9798865947615

Cover Design and Book Layout by Celina Duffy, Tagline Communications

Final Edit by Celina Duffy

In loving memory of Uncle James & Aunt Ora

ALTHEA JEWEL

ONE

I was outside. I thought I could've kept walkin' and then I realized he was right behind me. Off balance a split second, my shoe nicked the sprinkler's edge. I'd just bought those sneakers.

"Get back to where you come from," he yelled, "And GET that junk off my driveway!" Now it's personal. He didn't have to take it there. I clenched my teeth and turned to face him.

"Excuse me, SIR. This AIN'T nobody's junk!!" Back then teenagers didn't raise their voices to adults. What happened next felt like slow motion.

"BOY, if I say it's JUNK...that's what it is....Uh huh nothin' BUT..."

He lunged and I reacted. Spun him halfway around and he panicked. Then I landed a solid blow. Crimson blood streamed through the old man's teeth tricklin' down the side of his parched bottom lip. Mr. Whitfield's index finger swept over his mouth. Like I said, I was leavin'. But everybody knows.

There's history and there's his story. Peep this. So, if you can't beat somebody, you might resort to what Mr. Whitfield did. In that raspy hoarse voice of his, he served up profanities, gave me extras. Words he'd wanted to say to me all along.

Some tall guy...maybe in his 40's, had been watchin' from across the street, he walked over. "Hey. Hey, stop it!" Grabbed Mr. Whitfield's arm. "Bernie, Bernie, that's enough!" He took a long hard look at both of us. I was a disheveled wreck with blood on my hand.

Mr. Whitfield's lip was puffy and bruising up. The neighbor asked him, "Bernie, you alright?"

Those are the three words you never want to hear if you're in a fight. Your name, followed by "you alright" in a feel sorry for you tone. Mr. Whitfield, a respected man, had just been challenged by a teenager on his front lawn. You know, to be honest, I really didn't want to tag him. I didn't even know I had that much in me. But it had been building up over time. And today, it unleashed on my girlfriend's father. My son's grandfather, Bernard Whitfield.

The next thing his neighbor said..."Bernie, what got into you?"

"Ivan, call the cops, right NOW to get this punk off my property!!" Mr. Whitfield wrung his hands, straightened out his faded work shirt then nervously tucked the shirt back into his pants. Mr. Ainsworth knew. Fifty-something-year-old Whitfield had underestimated me.

Noisy crows flew overhead. They sounded off then scattered down the street. In disbelief of the confrontation, I raised my scooter onto the sidewalk, turned the key, wiped the handle bars and sped off. I was mad at myself for how I'd handled that whole scene. I went there in the first place to see Allison. She visits her parents often. I thought the baby wasn't due yet. None of this would've happened if I'd known Aaron was already born. I never thought we'd marry. Allison, or Alee, as everybody called her didn't love me.

Mr. Whitfield would probably rather die than to see his daughter change her last name to Morris. Well that didn't happen. Back then, only thing goin' my way was the weather. A sunny afternoon in Cerritos California. I was 19 but I didn't feel grown up. They say you're grown once you turn 18. That's like having a job for a year and expecting yourself to run the company, by yourself.

I grew up in a nice house. Well, considered nice, but modest. Ma liked it because of the brick trim. She had a knack for gardening. Collard greens, squash, and other vegetables out back. On the other hand, my father, loved the garage. He built shelves for his tools and kept his materials super organized.

During the week he worked 12 hours a day. But he relished his time on the weekends in his tool shed. His sanctuary. Pops friends would come over and they'd laugh and drink up his beer. But he didn't mind. His latest project was building baby cribs. He built a cool crib for me and Alee. It was almost finished.

As I wiped the sweat off my face and put the lock on my bike, Ma met me at the door through the garage. She always knew, even before I could say anything, "What happened to you?"

Trickles of his blood on my white T-shirt. "Ah, nothing, fell off my bike, I'm okay," I said quickly, headin' towards the front bathroom to clean up my mess.

She trailed off behind me, "I told you to be careful on that scooter."

I didn't want to add more to it so I changed the subject, "Ma, I need to see Alee, today." I took off my top T-shirt and balled it up, then adjusted the water in the sink.

"I thought that was where you just went to."

"No...I went over to the Whitfield's house. Ma she already had the baby...she's at the hospital." My mother didn't seem surprised, "Curtis, I wish you had come back last week."

"I talked to her a few days ago," I mumbled, "Baby wasn't due yet."

My mother wasn't having it, "She left a message here and I called you. Lorraine said you'd left for the airport."

"Why didn't you say something when I got here?"

"I was at the market when you got here Curtis...and by the time I got home you were gone."

"Besides," she went on, "You were supposed to be here last week."

"I didn't have the money last week!"

I hated when Ma was right and I was so terribly wrong. "We could have sent for you Curtis, all you had to do was ask."

Now I'm agitated. All this could've been avoided. I wanted to blame somebody besides me. But instead of saying that, I said, "I can't keep relying on everybody else to take care of my problems!"

"Don't use that tone with me," she rolled her eyes and said, "Curtis, you always have to learn the hard way, don't you?" She paused long and hard then said, "How long have we been telling you?"

I rinsed the soap off my shirt and kept quiet.

"If you don't want children, don't make no babies...no shells." Then she lowered her voice, "You hear me?"

With hands cupped under the running sink water, I apologized, "Yes ma'am." She stood silent in the hallway with her arms folded. I hated that. Her silence after putting me in check.

A soapy residue flowed down the drain. I rinsed out the sink and reached for my hand towel.

Ma added, "Fell down huh? Not in a fight?"

"Nope," I smiled, hopin' I could hide the truth and mask my adrenalin.

"Uh, huh," she mumbled something and walked away towards the kitchen.

I looked really hard in the mirror and asked myself... when am I going to get this right? I was crazy in love with Allison "Alee" Whitfield. She was everything I wasn't. She was outgoing and everybody wanted to be around her. She believed life was hers for the taking. And she was gorgeous. She had her mother's Native Indian features and her father's Black genes...the best of strength and beauty.

My mother was the oldest of thirteen kids, nine still living. Raised in Michigan. Back then, there was plenty work to go around. It was the late 60's. My grandpa was Joshua Frederick. Before he died, he assembled Town & Country station wagons for Chrysler Corporation. It was enough to pay the bills but nothing else. I heard things were going strong except for as Grandma Naomi called them "Papa's shells." Shells were his children conceived outside the marriage. Like sea shells. Tide rolls in. By nature, shells are buried in the sand. They yearn to be found or be thrown back into the ocean.

Ma, Claudia Lynn Frederick, started working at fifteen. She worked part-time and finished high school. She was a waitress in a busy restaurant across town. She loved herself in her own skin but said that as a dark-skinned woman she lost her tips to "high yellow" or "red-boned" girls, as they were called.

Her mother was a lighter complexion and it was a subtle but definite insecurity that she developed from a young age. But Ma is pretty. She captured the heart of twenty-two-year-old Wesley Morris with the first glance. There was no planned fancy romantic wedding. No down on one knee. No empty promises. I heard he just asked and she said one word, "Yes."

Ma stayed at the house after my sister Waleena was born. Then came me. She said she fell into a routine of watching soap operas like they were real people. As a kid, I didn't notice anything but my sister told me that our house felt like a soap opera. Our family was polite and kept on keepin' on but somethin' in my mother was missing. It finally came out. I remember an argument between my parents, well, she was the one yellin', "Wes, I can't do this anymore!"

One of her friends told her about learning to be a bartender on the weekends. "Girl, you need to get yourself a weekend hobby too."

I recalled her saying that to my mom. Under the circumstances, I thought it was pretty good advice. At first, pops flipped out, he was totally against it. That old, "What's best for the family," guilt trip. She stopped fussin' about it. She got back into her routine. It must have been on his conscious because one day, out of nowhere, my father gave Ma the green light.

"Claudia," he said apologizing, "Be a bartender, do whatever makes you happy."

That's all it took. We went from empty hollow to full and alive with Ma's confidence going through the roof. And she didn't miss a beat. We had three home cooked meals (as usual) and the house was lookin' like pages out of Good Housekeeping on the regular.

A few weeks later, I was ear hawkin' when Pops asked her, "How can you be a bartender and not drink?"

"A lot of us don't drink, Wes," she laughed, "That's how we give such good advice...you can't really hear people unless you're sober."

Wes trusted Ma. But he didn't trust those men waggin' their tongues and slappin' cash on the counter... winking at his wife. Now that I'm older I understand how he felt. Pops cleaned up after gettin' off his second job and put on a crisp shirt, no tie with a business jacket. Ha. Who did he think he was Miami Vice? He guarded Ma and crashed the bar for a couple months. For years Ma joked about what the owners said, "We have security Mr. Morris. Please, please go home."

Way before she started bartending, I remember walkin' home from the park with her. It was another warm day. She wore some just above-the-knee khaki shorts and a bright yellow tank top. Ma is top-heavy. Even when she doesn't try her blouse always fits tight. As it was, a couple of young guys, in their early twenties, were whispering, staring and commented about her chest.

I had to put my two cents in, "Say, don't be lookin' at my Mama like that!!" One of them said something smart and that was it! Barely 5 ft. 4, she took off her earrings, and pulled her hair back in a bun and proceeded to beat the crap out of one of those boys...the police came and everything! Those jokers went to jail and Ma dragged me by my earlobe yelling, "Curtis, don't you ever embarrass me like that again!"

I still laugh about that day. I was ready to fight but she put a move on him so quick, I just watched to see if that other cat was going to give me a reason to jump in. Don't underestimate Ma.

After I showered and trimmed up my sideburns, I put a load of clothes in the washer...including that shirt I'd saturated in the bathroom sink. Once I started the dryer, I found Ma, she was relaxin' on the sofa lookin' at our old baby photos.

"Ma you home tonight?" I said, touchin' her shoulder.

"No, it's slow at the bar, but I'm on the schedule tonight and tomorrow, why?"

"I want to know if I can borrow the car a few hours, to go see Alee and the baby."

"You did mention that earlier, huh?" She seemed to be in awe of a picture of Waleena at a track meet ceremony a few years back.

"Yea," I said. "I didn't want to bother you about it... but Ma, I really want to check on her."

"Okay sweetheart. Take the car. By the way, there's corned beef and cabbage on the stove." It smelled good but the last thing on my mind was food.

I headed out in Ma's station wagon to see Alee at Daniel Freeman Hospital. Lucky for me there wasn't a lot of traffic but it wasn't a hop-skip-jump across town. I did have some time to contemplate on a few things. I never thought Allison and I would be so far apart. But I couldn't find a decent job in L.A. It's hard enough with her being so difficult and thinking she knows so much. Add some distance and that makes it even harder.

But I was doing it to build somethin' for us for the future. She never thought about anything farther than what's directly in front of her. Some yakety-yak about living in the moment. That's how we ended up where we are today. But the baby, that's both of us not planning. I thought back to a conversation we had just a few months ago.

"Tell me, what you want me to do Alee?"

"Come back and take care of your responsibility." It's my fault...she always factored that in. Face scrunched and vein popping out my forehead, I yelled, "My responsibility?"

"Curtis, we made this baby together and now I'm doing all the..."

"Hold up now, you knew I moved to Atlanta...for our baby!!"

She cut me off, "We didn't decide to move, YOU decided!"

"Are you crazy? Stay in Los Angeles, no education, no skill and keep brawlin' with your father!"

"He said he would give you a job!" she shouted. I breathed heavily, "I don't need him to GIVE me a damn thing...you still don't get it?"

All 5 ft 7 inches of her caramel brown skin, drenched in emotion. She used those eyes. Motivate. Captivate. Even destroy if she had to. Her stare and his words if combined were enough to blow up a building without any dynamite. I'll never forget Mr. Whitfield calling me a Lying no good Negro living off welfare...and never been out of the ghetto...please tell your father I don't need his help.

Every mother across the globe will hate on me for saying this, but here it is. Men don't use intellect in bed. We're simple. It's an orgasm. We reach it. We take a breather, maybe even smoke a cigarette or a joint before we say anything. It's not that complicated. And NO, I'm not being insensitive.

And my right hand to God, I will never understand why women are so shocked when they tell us "I'm pregnant" and we don't react like we just won the six-hundred-million-dollar lottery or something.

I have strong beliefs. Astrology isn't one of them. But some of that stuff is for real. Alee, she's a cold Sagittarius, born on the 16th day of December. She won't compromise. Everything's her point-of-view. Don't trip. She's dealing. And don't worry about the cards...just play.

My entire family knew the Whitfields were trying to get the Morris' locked up or killed. Just speaking to their daughters was a crime. I never understood why. My parents owned their home and we'd been in the neighborhood for over fifteen years.

We went to the same schools. Shopped at the same stores; and when we got sick, the same doctors wrote our prescriptions. We buried our people in the same cemetery. Yet, they barely spoke to us on the street.

Once a year I visited my Uncle Joey in Georgia. I finally moved there to "get my stuff together" as Ma and Auntie Lorraine put it. Uncle Joey had his own business. He said a corporation would take a Black man in the

80's under three conditions: Number one, he couldn't look too Black. Not just skin tone but he had to watch his tone and be careful not to bring any attention to himself. Number two, he couldn't be too confident and don't be too friendly with the white girls (not in front of everybody). Pay close attention to number three. Number three, he couldn't plan to pass anything down to the next generation. A contingency plan with no legacy.

Uncle Joey taught me how to run a business. We got our share of callouses and body aches but we were making lots of cash. Never had to look down when I wanted to look up, wore my confidence on the outside, and didn't kiss anybody's butt for anything.

"What's Allison saying about your plans to build her a house?" I buttoned up my work shirt, "Aww no, my little shack...not big enough for Queen Anne." Uncle Joey's wife Lorraine, known as Rain, poured half-and-half into her cup and stirred it gently.

"Hahahaha," she laughed, "You can build a few houses on this land compared to California." I grinned but made no comment.

Then she asked me, "Where you say her people are from?"

Uncle Joey chimed in, "Chicago...the south side."

Auntie added, "Hmm, I guess they're important now...movie stars...Black gold and Texas tea, just like the Beverly Hillbillies."

"Not Ellie Mae but Alee Mae." I added. We all laughed out loud on that one.

Aunt Lorraine was comfortable in her own skin. She didn't look it but she was close to fifty, and my uncle was fifteen years younger. Lorraine smiled before placing a steaming pan of hash browns in the center of the table. She commented, "I was just looking at a picture of you and Alee, you all are such a cute couple," she paused then said, "When is she coming here to visit?"

"Now Rain, we're all family, but let Curtis handle his business."

I scarfed down scrambled eggs and a heaping of parmesan grits. "You sure know how to cook auntie!"

"Thank you, ya'll need to eat right to do a good job out there..."

That was the routine for the 6 ½ months. Right around that time, we were just finishing breakfast, the phone rang. Aunt Rain answered.

"Hello." My uncle cleared his throat as she passed me the phone.

"Hello, oh Traci...what's going on?"

"Alee said if you can't make it next week, don't come back, period," she laughed sarcastically.

"Aww no, you're joking, right?"

"I tried talking some sense in her Curtis, you know she's stubborn."

"Yea, I know."

"She doesn't appreciate you," Traci whispered.

"Why are you whispering?"

Traci Whitfield rushed our brief talk. "Got to go, I'll talk to you later."

"Wait, Trace, did you give her the money?"

"Yes, I did."

I had been sending Alee money, every month. Half of our savings. The other half in a bank account here in Atlanta. I sent her cashier's checks. I thought that would show her I meant business. Found out down the line, she hardly ever opened mail from me. It was like she wanted people to think I was no good.

Ten minutes later my uncle was ready to go, "Curtis, let's get a move on."

Uncle Joey kissed his wife on the cheek and she waved while closing the screen door behind us. Aunt Lorraine had a super clean Fleetwood Cadillac. It was parked out front like a show car. We rode in his work truck that I nicknamed "Sprinter" because it was more reliable short distances. First, after he gave it a little gas, it rolled backwards, even when we were not on a hill.

First day in the truck I had a panic attack. I wanted to scream but I couldn't conjure one up. Before I could react Sprinter would take off somewhere between first and second gear...and the rest was easy. More or less.

My uncle's nemesis was his sinus condition. It was so annoying. He probably could have corrected it with some type of treatment but he'd suffered so long it became a habit. He snorted dry and loud then waited for the truck to warm up. After a week, I just got used to it. He popped a peppermint candy in his mouth and waved to Mr. Rhodes, his neighbor down the street.

Alee told me she had trust issues with men. Her past relationships overlapped ours. I believe some of that is true. But I know for a fact, she brought that up to her benefit. When things got tough and she didn't want to work it out with me.

I would never lay a hand on her or any woman. But she said it was the emotional abuse that cut her the deepest. Like, she already expects men to let her down. I was hoping to be different. Maybe I just didn't try hard enough. But right now, here I am walkin' towards the entrance to Daniel Freeman Hospital in Inglewood, California to see her and my son. And then it hits me.

The last time I'd been to a hospital was to say goodbye to my sister before she passed away. It didn't occur to me that comin' here to welcome a child into this world would bring about a past memory of going to the hospital to watch someone die. Superman, my ass. Shit hit me like kryptonite. I know it was emotion. But real talk, my chest, my back, all the way up to my shoulder, I felt a surge of tightness. I stepped out of the elevator, faced the closest wall, bowed my head, and prayed.

God please take this terrible weirdness away and give me strength to move forward. I took a deep breath and walked to the nurses station, face flushed, but smiled and then asked to see my son, Baby boy Whitfield. I was given a hospital gown and then led to the nursery.

"Hold him, he won't break," the nurse smiled. I never felt nervous about holdin' him. I was like every other father, filled with pride.

He was perfect. All six pounds eleven ounces. My man child. God had entrusted his life to me. He was wrapped in a warm blue-and-white blanket. I loosened it a tiny bit and whispered a prayer in his ear. He studied me. It was as if he had been waitin' for me to show. His eyes seemed focused on the hair above my lip. "Whatcha think? Should I shave it off," smiling about my moustache..."I thought it made me look cool but whatever you want little man."

Ma always said every generation of babies gets smarter. I couldn't believe that a newborn could look at me with such intensity. Maybe just my conscious but it felt like he wanted to say, so what are you going to do now. For now, he has my dark brown eyes, a little bit slanted just like hers. But his most prominent feature is his nose, keen and bold. A trademark of sorts passed down from generations of Morris men.

As I admired him, I noticed the oval shaped birthmark on his left cheek, just like mine. I watched him until he fell back asleep. I had waited too long to be near him and I wasn't gonna leave the nursery, at least not right away. Today, March 12, 1982, I stopped being afraid of hospitals. At least in this moment. The nurses let me sit down and keep holdin' him.

As I gently rocked him I thought about last winter. And the letter I wrote to his mother.

As Salaam Alaikum, My Queen.

I wanted you to know that I can keep my promises (smiles). Uncle Joey says you can stay in the spare room. I love you. And miss you.

P.S. I hope you are not still mad. I know it must be hard on you and I don't want to upset you on the phone because they say it can affect the baby. I am going to be a good father. Okay? So, here's your ticket, and $200.00 to buy whatever you need to get ready for the trip. One more thing, I want you to reconsider giving our baby a Muslim name.

See you soon. Take care.

Always and forever, Curtis Kareem

That was December 1st.

I called to see if she got my mail and Mr. Whitfield, as expected hung up on me.

Then I called Traci, "Hey."

"Hey."

"Tell your pops to stop hangin' up on me. I just need to know did Alee get my letter."

"Uh huh," she whispered, "I gave it to her. She's taking a nap right now."

"What did she say about comin' out here? Did she mention the money to you?"

"Oh yea, she got it."

"I just want everybody to know that I take care of mines, you know."

"Yeah, I know."

"Let her know I called."

"I will Curtis, you take care."

"Thanks sis, I knew I could count on you." I stopped callin' the Whitfields after Traci assured me that Alee was planning to come see me. I imagined her comin' out here and wantin' to stay in Atlanta, at least until the baby is born.

And then the day came for her to fly out.

The weatherman threatened nothing but gloom. It was gonna be cold. Cold enough for us to feel the frostbite on our behinds...mine was frozen. The airport was packed. The holiday travelers were ready. Long coats, extra layers of clothing, winter hats and gloves. I was wearing my warmest dark brown slacks and my tan winter coat and hat. Alee said I looked good in tan. I parked in the public lot and hustled past the taxis and people on-the-move.

A slender young woman with a newborn walked towards me, she smiled and walked past. I was gettin' anxious. My gut said that there was somethin' wrong; but I pushed that thought aside.

I glanced at my watch again... I was a little early and with the extra time I sat alongside the terminal and waited. After the last passenger came out the gate I started to panic. Did I miss something or did she miss her flight? I confirmed with the desk, no stragglers.

"Yes, everyone's exited the plane." I'd lost hope until I noticed someone waving at me to get my attention.

"Alee!" I shouted, waving back at her. I walked briskly towards the girl wearing a red coat with black fur trim, but as I got closer...it was...not Allison but Traci that met me.

"Where's Alee?" I said, then looked behind Traci in a crowd of people without greeting her.

Traci took the hood off her parka and said, "She's not coming."

"What?" I shouted, "What, she missed the flight, why didn't she call?" I get it, Alee hates talkin' on the phone, but this is just plain ridiculous.

"Ah, Curtis, maybe we should sit down a minute."

At that moment I imagined the worst...what happened, was she sick, she's pregnant..."Is the baby alright?"

Traci had a small overnight bag on her shoulder. She set the bag down and removed her gloves. The suspense was killing me. In hindsight, I should've left her ass in the airport, right then, but I took the bait. She opened her purse and pulled out this fat envelope, sighed, "No. She's fine Curtis...here."

"Traci! What the hell?"

Before social media, people were ruining lives with their cameras...hard copy evidence in your face. I looked at the first pic. Alee with her hair all down sexy and straight. The side of her face, touching the side of some freckled face pale white boy's cheek. This chump is looking like, "I can't wait to sex-this-one-more-time." That's where my imagination went. My pregnant girlfriend cheating on me. The only thing lower is me cheating on my pregnant girlfriend.

I wanted to go find this cat and feed him to a coyote. I'm busting my ass and she's messin' around with some goofy white boy with my baby in her belly!

"Traci, did you fly all the way down here just to muck with me, or what?" My eyes watered with anger and disbelief. I waited for her to say something.

"I couldn't tell you this over the phone. I tried to tell you but...I..." My voice cracked, "How long has this been going on?"

"Curtis, I'm I'm...I am so sorry," she stuttered.

In a mad rage I searched for a pay phone. "Let's call Miss Alee right now!" I snatched the top two photographs and threw the rest back towards her face as she watched seemingly afraid and said, "No telephone there. They went to his parent's cabin for the weekend."

"Trace, you can take this bullshit with you on the next flight back to L.A. NOW!" An Asian couple looked at me as though I'd lost my mind. Maybe I had.

I walked away from the crowd to an empty row of chairs diagonal from the window. I sat motionless, staring into empty space while airplanes moved in and out of the airport. Traci waited about ten minutes before approaching me, cryin' and said, "Curtis, just listen a minute."

"I thought I told you to get lost," I said in an angry tone.

She moved closer to me, "I know you don't believe me, but I told her to tell you." It was as if a trap door opened and I fell, head first, right into it.

I threw my coat over my shoulder and said, "Let's go find a bar." She followed me and halfway smiled.

"The sooner I get drunk, the better," I forced a laugh.

I downed so many shots I lost count. I paid for the liquor and she bought the food. I guess it's true what they say, misery loves company. But they didn't say keep company with the devil's daughter. I must've missed that part.

ALTHEA JEWEL

TWO

Then my dumb ass apologized. "I'm sorry I yelled at you Trace. This isn't me. I don't know who I am anymore."

"I understand," she smiled, patting my shoulder.

Some random girl grabbed my hand and we started dancing. Traci was somewhere on the dance floor but I wasn't really keepin' up with her. Half the night passed and when I woke up, I was half naked, wearin' my shirt but no pants. Daylight peeked through the blinds. Traci all up in my face. She reached for me and I withdrew from her touch.

"Looks like somebody had too much to drink, huh?" People say, I was drunk and it just happened. I honestly don't remember the act, but I acknowledge the pain I felt and the pain I caused because of my actions. Alcohol, like any drug, can only temporarily disguise the truth but it cannot drown your reality.

Today, three months later, I still ask myself that question. Why did I ruin my chance of happily ever after by involving myself in that scandalous bullshit? It's hard enough, being a good parent without any drama. Holdin' my son makes me remember my indiscretion. And now, on a day when the future should be looking bright, and lookin' like the beginning, it almost feels like the end. And peep this, I'm the only one who is still hurting.

When I was in middle school, I liked basketball but I loved running. My sister already had the track and field mindset and then we both joined a team. Our folks were super supportive.

"Wally..."

"Yeah Ma, I'm almost ready!"

"Girl, you can clean that room when we get home... let's go!" Ma slapped her hands together, as if that would make Sis move any faster.

I was already in the back seat of our dusty 1970 sky blue station wagon. It was just transportation. Waleena was the original OCD. She rarely left home until everything in proximity was orderly and accounted for. I swore she had a checklist.

"Okay Ma, coming!" She jetted to the car with back pack, cleats strung over her shoulder, munching on a breakfast snack in her free hand.

Ma adjusted the rear view and Waleena jumped in the front passenger seat. "Boy, what you lookin at?"

"Almost late again, because of you, fat head," I laughed. Ma was asking Waleena if she'd taken her medication but Sis wasn't paying attention.

"Did you hear me?" Ma mumbled something, as she drove through the next intersection. Waleena rolled down her window and looked away from Ma's face.

"I took them! I hate being reminded every morning on the way to school that I'm dying!" Ma swerved the car inches from the curb and then slammed on the brakes.

"Don't you dare talk to me in that tone!" Ma's eyes were glaring in what appeared to be anger. Ma was just afraid. Quietest kept, we all were. The front car windows started to fog up. Ma turned on the defrost. Most times I was so scared I thought that maybe we should turn around and go back home. There would be no U-turns today. Or any day. We moved forward. That was all we knew to do.

Cerritos was a pretty chill city. A lot of trees and landscaping. It was once a farmland, "Dairy Valley" they called it. A small city with a shopping center on Del Amo Boulevard. The people who lived here were mostly Hispanic, some White people, and Asians with sprinkles of Black people.

A few minutes later we drove up to the field. Leena blew her nose and quickly shook it off. I gave her a reassuring nod and put on my cleats. Ma sat behind the other parents on one of the top bleachers. We ran our laps until the fog surrendered to welcome us with sunlight.

"You think Ma is losing it?" My sister paused, breathing heavily and waited for me to answer. I didn't answer. I just smiled and got in position to run another lap.

Adrenalin on point and my calf muscles felt stronger than ever as I passed her on the last leg to the finish line. A split-second behind me Leena sped up and high-fived my unofficial victory. "Big head, you might make All-City like me someday!"

"Yea," I smiled back at her. "I just might make it."

Way before Alee and me started dating, our families knew of each other. We lived in close proximity. Less than two miles away. The Whitfields and the Morris' were neighborly. Mrs. Whitfield and Lorraine were chopping it up, you know, conversating...and after they went back home, Ma and auntie kept talkin' while I practiced free-throws on the hoop in our backyard.

"Kaye asked me if we're movin' in with you and Wes," Auntie laughed.

"What?" Ma looked surprised.

"She made it a point to tell me that they were the first Black family to purchase a home in this neighborhood," Auntie smiled and sipped her soda.

"Like we can't afford to buy a house on our own, or maybe you needed us to move in to make ends meet."

"That witch!" Ma shouted out. Aunt Rain is part-Cherokee and said that Kaye Whitfield kept braggin' about it.

"That woman made me not want to claim having a drop, not one drop of Indian blood."

"Rain what did she say?"

"She started talkin' that spooky junk and asking me if I wanted one of her trinkets, for good luck."

"Luck?" Ma added, "She's lucky that man married her crazy ass." Ma and auntie laughed so hard, auntie's hip hurt, and Ma's eyes filled with tears.

Those were happy times. I did what normal kids do. School. Homework. Playtime. I remember when me and Leena were talkin' about when-we-grow-up-and-get-married...

Leena had the car that day and we took off to watch another track event. "Who you gonna marry Leena?" She smiled and struck a pose.

"Married?" she shot back, "Not doing that! Babies give you stretch marks all the way down to your feet," she laughed, "No way Jose...I won't ever get married!" All she wanted was to get to the NCAA competition. But you have to finish state before nationals.

It was a real hot afternoon in the valley. Almost 90 degrees. We rested our backs against the top bleachers where we could see the best contenders. Waleena spotted some friends and went over to chit chat. I hung out for a while on my own.

She came back later all excited, "Do you know who that was?"

"Nope," I answered nonchalantly, "Who?"

"College boys, from Cal State, they want me to come to their meet...they think I can qualify."

"Qualify? Qualify for what?"

I gazed near the front row at two skinny tall brothers...gawking up and drooling over my sister. She looked down and waved back at them, one with the CSUN shirt and shorts waved back. "He looks like a surfer, not a track star, Leena?" I took a long sigh.

"He's on the A list, All-City," she boasted. It got interesting. See, I thought I was gifted at thirteen when my voice changed. On that particular day, I was sixteen. My baritone was sexy or threatening...depending on how I used it. I ain't nobody's cello. I stared them down with my hardest expression and said hello.

"Curtis! Why'd you do that?"

"Do what?" I smirked, almost laughing.

"Always talking mean and running my friends off!!"

"Girl please, how could I scare off a grown ass man from, who'd you say, Cal State?"

Next to my sister's first love for track and field was education. She knew her sciences. Biology, Anatomy, and Physiology. I never was much of a buff but destiny nudged me to study my own history. It started kind of subtle. A year prior, in my freshman year in high school, we both gravitated to learn about African and Egyptian history.

It was a popular theme to wear a lot of black. I had a green, black, and red Dashiki, to represent the power base of Africa. I had a lot of Black pride. I grew an Afro to acknowledge my respect for the motherland. My "fro" was clean. I learned a little Swahili and some Arabic over the popular French and Spanish electives of my peers. I studied a book about Egyptian symbols. I always believed that symbolism, in its right context, can teach us the meaning of life.

I felt a connection with "Shenu" also known as Shen. It was a cool looking symbol too. I was hyped about gettin' a "Shen" tattoo on my right arm. Mainly because only a few cats in our neighborhood even had tattoos. And so, one Saturday afternoon, I begged Leena to borrow the car and take me to a tattoo shop. "You didn't tell me it was all the way by Venice Beach!"

"Calm down Leena. I got your gas money on the way back."

The ocean water looked like a kaleidoscope of shimmering diamonds. I mean, it was awesome that day. She was doing that big sister attitude thing. But after I got mine, I convinced her to get a matching one.

"It's perfect!" she finally said eyeing the handy work on her upper left arm. She didn't flinch or complain about feelin' any pain.

"Yep," she smiled, "Perfect, just like we wanted, huh?"

The quarter-sized circle resembled the sun. The sun which for many civilizations, generations before us, was how we told time. This sun disc symbolized eternal life. The sun, the moon, and the stars were not just nature's beauty they were protectors of man and God's creation. The line at the base is called "Maat" which stands for truth and balance.

"Curtis?"

"What?"

"How long before Ma beats us down over these tattoos?" I shrugged my shoulders but didn't answer her.

She admired her tattoo proudly, "You're right, it's not like Ma can tell us to take them back."

Every family has a story about some type of homemade contraption that siblings have crafted into a crazy invention. I must've been nine or maybe even ten-years-old. Our dad, Wesley Morris worked long days. On top of that a full eight every Saturday, on his building projects, for as long as I can remember. He could fall asleep waiting in line in the grocery store. Ma would nudge him before his snoring got too loud. I got the feelin' she had to do that a lot. I'm surprised the neighbors didn't throw empty bottles and bricks through their bedroom window. As young kids, Waleena and I tried an experiment to solve his snoring problem.

"Shhh."

"Stop shhishing me Leena."

"Curtis, be quiet!" Hunched down near the wall next to the vintage wall clock. I remembered being petrified of the snoring overlapping the ticking clock. We crawled alongside an imaginary Ninja trail towards dad's bellowing snores...straight into the den where dad was asleep on his leather recliner.

"What do we do now?"

"Shhh."

I blinked my eyes, irritated by her bossy manner, but I was down for the challenge. She named it the "EZ Sleep Pin" an old stretched out headband and two glued on clothes pins. I folded over the strips of duct tape onto the headband. And she crazy glued the pins. It looked like a 1950's makeshift monster headset. Amateurs but proud of our creation.

In theory, as a child, it seemed brilliant. In reality, it was a disaster waitin' to happen. We eased the contraption on pop's nose and voila, no snoring for a few minutes and then he choked violently. EZ Pin still in place, he woke and saw us standing over him...Leena froze and I took off. I never made it out the front door.

Pops exhaled and then it came. Coughin', more chokin', and to our surprise he removed the headset and started laughing. I couldn't believe we didn't get in any trouble. Those were happy times. Family trouble didn't start until Leena, a junior in high school, was diagnosed with cancer. She never looked sick...for almost a year we thought she was going to beat it. She dropped out of the track team because her energy was too low. But down the line we ran practice relays just like the old days. It seemed to help her. Stay active and live or slow down and die. Before she came home from her chemo treatments, I would straighten up her room, dust, and put fresh sheets on her bed. I even folded her laundry, sometimes. I pulled some flowers from out front and put them in one of the crystal vases from Ma's china cabinet.

"You alright Curtis...you know that?"

"Yea Leena, I know."

I remember when my father told me what I didn't want to hear. It was a couple weeks before Thanksgiving. If you ask me, it might as well have been three weeks to the end of the world. Pops was in the garage, sanding off some wood work. He set his materials down next to him on the bench and looked up to me. "Your sister is not well," he spoke just above a whisper. I blinked, paused, still standing there...motionless.

"Curtis, we have to take Leena back to the hospital."

THREE

I take issue with how people say, so-and-so lost their battle with cancer. I get it that you're in a fight. The fight of your life. But on the field, even if you can't see your opponent, at least you should be able to estimate, calibrate, and with some type of precision to know when to strike.

On the ground. And from distances away from the battlefield. Yea, I guess estimates are the different stages. And the therapy is somewhat calibration. But if science is so much less predictable than war…and it works for some and not for others…then I don't call that a fair fight. Let me say this. I don't question man's mortality. And I don't question God's dominion...

November 30, 1980, Waleena Morris, my only sibling, ended her journey. She was 18. I wouldn't say she lost her battle with cancer. She never gave up. We, the family, the friends, the doctors…lost her. I'm reminded daily of all she stood for. Mature beyond her years. I will never forget her. I look at my tattoo and cherish our day at Venice Beach, and how, together, we became warriors.

When I met Alee, or rather, when she acknowledged me, I was infatuated. As I said before, we Morris' were friendly with the Whitfield family. I didn't admire her from a far or anything like that. But she obviously didn't pay me no mind. She must've forgotten that we were neighbors. But anyway, while I pursued her, I was still processing the loss of my sister. My emotions were opened up.

Alee will say that I lied to her about my age. Well, that's not completely true. At first, before she got pregnant, she just didn't ask. Besides, I was only three years younger than her. That's like a freshman dating a senior. I was 18 and she was 21. That type of shit only mattered when you are in high school. But she was always over the top and made a big deal out of it.

I was unofficially workin' with my Uncle Joey and when the baby was on the way, that job became official. As soon as our son, Aaron was born, Allison Nicole Whitfield gave back her labor pains to me.

It was another chill day in Los Angeles. The cab drove through downtown and I gazed up at a few tall buildings, seemed too close together. By the time we got to the airport, I focused on how can I make more money to raise my child. Cars were movin' almost on each other's bumpers. Horns blowing.

Today, I just wanted to get back to work…back to ATL. The flight was alright. No turbulence. No terrorist. No problem. I had been reclining. I moved my seat back up, to be more alert. She was making her last rounds.

"Can I get you anything?"

"Yea, do I have to show some ID?"

"No sir," she laughed flirtatiously then winked at me before servin' me a double whisky. To be honest, I didn't much care for scotch. I just thought it made me look more grown up.

Uncle Joey signed us to a new job. We were so busy that before I knew it the year was almost over. My body was tired. I took a long shower then watched a little television. All channels seemed to be saying the same theme. Spend. Put it on your credit card and defer for one year…but spend it.

I turned the set off and listened to the stereo. Auntie came downstairs and sat down at the end of the sofa. By now I was stretched out coddling a forget-about-it cocktail, admiring their flock white tree.

"Anything under there for me?" she smiled, gazing at the assortment of colorful Christmas presents.

"I thought ya'll put all this stuff under here for me!" I laughed.

"You celebrating Christmas now?" she chuckled.

"No ma'am. I don't celebrate much of anything anymore."

Uncle Joey always wrapped the presents. They were too perfect…almost seemed like he used a measuring tape and a ruler. He took pride in everything he did. Besides building houses, and fixin' things, he loved wrapping gifts. He said it took his mind off big jobs to focus, even if only for a moment, on a task like this…he was pretty darn good at it too.

Aunt Lorraine interrupted my awkwardness. "Made pound cake, want to have some with me?" I grinned, then high fived her. She brought two saucers and two forks into the front room.

"Thank you."

"Sure sweetheart, how is Allison doing?"

"She's alright, I guess."

She paused a moment glanced at the decorated tree, then back at me. "How's the baby?"

"Growing," I smiled proudly.

"You think she will let us keep him for a while down here?"

I didn't have to think about it, "Probably not."

"She would if you'd ignore the rest of them."

"What do you mean?" I asked intently.

"Allison's people call the shots..."

I finished my cake. "Large and in charge."

"Well, we just have to be smarter," she chuckled, "Bigger they are the harder they fall." I shook the ice in my glass beginning to feel a little mellow.

"Curtis, I've been in love with Joey since I first met him. He's a lot younger than me."

"Oh, I didn't know auntie you look so young."

She laughed, "It's true. Nothing but a number...Men miss out, looking for a woman in a girl. You are an exceptional young man and very mature. Find you a real woman." I sobered up a bit and I guess I never thought about it like that.

Then she asked me about my sister's room. "Your mother has Leena's room made up...like she's still here. Everything is just where it was."

I couldn't even bear to say it. "It's...like time stood still or something."

I closed my eyes picturing the bright pink theme in Sis' hollow bedroom.

Auntie continued, "No parent expects their child to leave this earth before them."

I tried to put myself in Ma's shoes. My voice cracked, "The room thing it shouldn't be that way."

"Talk to your father about it. Offer him your support on changing up that room."

I was makin' steady money. My uncle told me to set up different accounts. "One in your name and a college fund for Aaron."

Instead of mailing her checks, which she claimed never arrived. To stay out of court, I wired child support, on the 1st...and on the 15th a separate one to his college fund, so Alee couldn't touch it.

Pops said Ma was going to need more time to do anything about the room. She was on prescription medication and supposed to start counseling, which she was putting off.

"Okay pops. You let me know if anything changes. Joey and me can come knock down a wall and enlarge the room, and maybe put a skyline in it."

It was starting to depress me. I felt guilty for being away from my dad and my son. They both needed me and I was not around. I wanted to just forget about everything for a while. I wanted to get laid. I never had any problems with the ladies. I met a few girls, women rather, to help me blend in and give the appearance that I doing well for a youngster.

"Yolanda!" I hugged her with one arm, and secured the crinkled paper bag with a 5th of gin in my left hand. She was divorced. No children. Her house was built in the late 50's and it was immaculate. I liked to let the light in. I'd open the blinds, she'd close them.

"Hey baby!" she exhaled a puff of smoke from her cigarette, "You been working hard?"

One night she put on a leopard print gown and some glass slippers. She grabbed my crouch, untied my pants and forced the length of me, almost completely down her juicy throat... nobody ever did me like that and I was hooked on this twenty-nine-year-old gangster Latina love.

Yolanda met my physical needs but nothing more. I was not in love with her...she wasn't lookin' for love. Just some young stud to show up late Friday night and leave before Sunday. I would shower and be gone, sometimes without even saying goodbye.

Yolanda was fair skinned with chestnut-brown curly hair and freckles. She was fine. But I never felt connected to her. To be honest, I should've seen that she was wantin' more than just a physical relationship. Don't get me wrong, we won't turn down oral sex but if you're not gettin' much in return, it should tell you something. I didn't promise her anything, so I felt comfortable enough to see two other chicks on the side. Debbie Payne was no pain and Tanya, her best friend loved to get freaky with a brother...anywhere I wanted.

"Curtis, where's your Yo Yo?" both girls giggled, "Can you pick us up outside in front of the dorm?"

First lesson: Don't tell chick numbers two and three about number one.

"Tanya!" I planted a wet kiss on her cheek, "Missed you ladies!"

Debbie had mad love for me but I just used her when I got bored with Tanya.

"Curtis," she whispered, "I've been keepin' it hot just for you."

Tanya turned up the radio as it sounded off Billy Paul's Me and Mrs. Mrs. Jones...I remember her very well. Tanya Campbell, a cute twenty-two-year-old college sophomore, had a small frame and a big Southern behind. She wore her hair pinned up sometimes in a school teacher bun...said she had been wearing her hair like that since Catholic school. I got a hard on just thinking about it.

"Yeah," she said, grinning at the bulge in my pants.

I didn't love her either but the whistle hadn't blown yet. So, I was still in the game. After I lost Alee, I just didn't care. But I had enough sense to use protection this time around. I kept a grip of K-jelly and condoms on hand. I had learned my lesson on that. Unfortunately, that isn't all a man should consider.

"How do you want it Curtis, baby?"

"Sit on top...and bend your legs back towards me." I positioned her legs, gently pulled them at my side, and watched her, toes curled, while she held on until she couldn't take it no more. She sat straight down on the pony. Aww yeah. I felt her vagina grippin' me with sheer wet pleasure. And that made me stand up even harder. Tanya had a thing with the position. She could bounce with it front or back opposite me, cowgirl style. I bounced her right back, up-and-down, slow, fast, any way she wanted it.

"Oh Curtis, you're gonna make me come!!!"

"Turn over girl," I said boldly.

I caressed her body sideways. As my passion grew she climaxed. I felt her motion towards me as I pressed on inside of her...tappin' her behind with the palms of my hands while I penetrated her...a few more strokes for good measure.

We lay in the hotel bed motionless for a long while, before either of us could speak. "You want some more?" I taunted her.

"Curtis, you tryin' to kill me, I can't take no more." Looking back, I was a playing a dangerous game. You see, I thought being involved with more than one woman at a time certified or rather qualified me as untouchable. Even a spider can spin a web to catch a bug for his dinner. But sometimes, that same spider will spin that web even tighter around himself.

FOUR

"Hello, can I speak with Tanya?"

"This is Tanya."

"My name is Yolanda."

"Yolanda?" Tanya was puzzled for a minute.

"I'm Curtis Morris' woman."

"How did you get my number?" Yolanda began to fidget, uncomfortable but kept talkin', "That's not important right now...the point is I want you to leave my man alone!"

"Oh, okay," Tanya laughed, "Should I tell Debbie to leave him alone too?"

"Who the hell is Debbie?"

Tanya changed the momentum, "Look, you sound like a nice lady," she paused, "But you don't know Curtis like I do."

"What do you mean by that?" By the time Tanya and Debbie got through talking to Yolanda her brain was fried. Little did I know until I saw Yolanda the next day.

"Hey baby." Yolanda's greenish-grey eyes dilated, "Sit down Curtis, we need to talk."

I remember takin' off my jacket and easin' my behind on the sofa. It was so sudden. A tiny knot grew large in my stomach. All men know that when a woman says we need to talk…it's definitely an intro to bad news.

My bicep tightened as I held onto the flowers that I'd brought her. "I had a talk with a female friend of yours, earlier today."

The flowers slipped from my hand and were face down on the coffee table next to me.

I listened. "Her name is Tanya. You left her phone number in your uniform pocket."

Tears began to fill her eyes and she said, "I probably shouldn't be doing YOUR DIRTY laundry anyway."

"Yoli…" she cut me off, "Let me finish!"

"I don't understand how you could humiliate me like this, why?"

I sat very, very still and listened while that nervous vein in my forehead pulsated.

"You made a fool of me, what did I do to deserve this Curtis, what?"

"Damn Yoli! I said I'm sorry!"

"Sorry?" she mumbled in Spanish profanities, and threw the flowers in my face.

"You're only sorry that I found out!"

She was right. I thought I had another quarter to play. But the game was over. I grabbed her and held her tightly, apologized, but it was too late. Damaged and beyond trustin' me again, she cried uncontrollably.

"Curtis, you never wanted me…I am not stupid…I wanted you! I loved you!"

When I do stupid things, I immediately search my soul for answers. We Morris' were brought up Baptist. I was dipped in the water and covered with the blood long before I knew how to say "I'm saved."

Growing up, we lived in church. Christianity was a chore. Pastor wanted money to buy this and that, and we just didn't have it. One day they passed the offering plate "three times" and my father put a $50 bill in, stood up, walked out, and hasn't been back to the Lord's house since. Later on, we heard him tell Ma, "No disrespect to Jesus, but I can't buy my way into heaven!"

I was sixteen when I met my best friend from the old neighborhood. Ahmad Muhammad was a Muslim from birth. He spoke fluent Arabic and prayed five times a day. His parents were always home when he got out of school so I spent most of my time at Ahmad's house. They claimed me as family and I learned to pray in Arabic and fasted during the holy month of Ramadan. They even named me, Curtis "Kareem" Muhammad.

I learned a lot from Ahmad. He was tall, slender, and sort of goofy but smart as a whip. He had a mad crush on my sister. One time I had to set him straight. He wasn't just admiring her...he was head-to-toe checking her out. She was wearin' white shorts and a fitted T-shirt...I told him we're brothers, and "our sister" better stay off the radar or I would have to kick his Saudi behind!

Otherwise, I had no qualms about Brother Ahmad. My introduction to Islam taught me another important life's lesson, on dealing with Mr. Whitfield. One day after school Ahmad and I were joggin' home and one of his shoe laces came untied. We stopped momentarily for him to lace it up.

"You have to learn how prejudice works," he said calmly.

"Just like these tennis shoes," he said. "I can't walk much less run with them untied."

I was jogging in place gettin' impatient with him, "Come on man, no sermon today."

"Kareem, you think the field is level don't you?" I really didn't know what he was talking about.

"What field? Man you always talkin' in riddles!"

"Allah u Akbar!" he shouted and laughed, "Straight talk is to a wise man, as a riddle is to a fool."

We walked side by side continuing our convo. "Kareem, you must see the world from the big picture…no one said that life will be right, reasonable, or fair…if I am running without tying my laces I can trip —maybe even fall."

He went on to say, "When things are not properly tied, or fitting in your life," he tied his shoe laces for emphasis, "First… tie them back up."

He stood back up on the sidewalk next to me and gave me a minute to think. "The Whitfield's insult you to get a reaction out of you…and the reaction they anticipate will make you trip…"

Ahmad was the brother I never had. We looked out for each other. We kept it real and I could talk to him about anything. Even after I moved to Georgia we stayed in touch. I was not surprised to hear from him when he called my Uncle J's house to check on me.

"As Salaam Alaikum."

"Salaams, my Brother!" I laughed, "I was just thinking about you."

"Kareem, you were in L.A. and didn't bother to look up your extended family?"

I had been trying so hard to work things out that I hadn't taken time out to call him. "Aww man, you know I had to see my son, Marsha-Allah, time just got away from me."

"You fasting next week?"

"I didn't know it was next week, wow, where have I been?" I said, embarrassed.

"Same ole' same ole' Kareem," he chuckled, "When the moon is sighted I will call and let you know."

It was a while since I had been involved in the community. At first, my uncle wasn't too keen on me taking an hour off in the middle of every Friday for prayer, so I saved and got my own transportation. It was an older model four door Buick Regal. And it was clean! The back door to the driver side was kinda stuck, but I loved my dark brown with tan interior vehicle. It had really low miles on it, and it was practically a steal $1950.00…cash.

The second week of Ramadan I met a lady at the Muslim restaurant named Jasmine. She was standing at the counter lookin' at the menu when I walked in. We greeted, I thought to myself, what a beautiful sister. Then I waited for the waitress to find me a table.

Somehow, they seated me before they took care of her, and I thought that was odd. So, I asked the waitress to offer Jasmine my table; or better yet, to join me. Elegant Jasmine, with her mystique and confident walk, approached me. I scrambled to stand up and offered her my seat.

"Al-Hamdullilah. Looks like you were here before me," I grinned, "Please, My Queen, have a seat…I'll wait for the next table."

"No thank you," she smiled, "That is very generous of you, Brother, ah."

"Brother Kareem," I smiled, finally we were talking. "And you are?"

"Jasmine." As I hoped there was chemistry between us. "I ordered to go, but thank you for offering."

She walked back to the counter space and waited three or so more minutes. Now it was apparent that Jasmine had nowhere to stand even to wait for her order. I insisted she take my seat. We both saw how quickly the restaurant filled, reluctantly, she sat down.

By tradition, she didn't make eye contact with me. She diverted her gaze on food being served or the continuous line of people adjacent to our small table. I was mesmerized by her clothing. She wore a beige silk garment and pearls. A beautiful hijab covering her hair. Her skin was flawlessly gorgeous with no makeup.

An older man served us iced water, "Have you ordered?"

"Yes sir, but this sister placed an order first, can you check on that please?"

When something goes wrong at a place of business, even in a restaurant, I would begin to be annoyed by bad service. But Sister Jasmine's patience seemed to calm me. Our waitress, Rasheeda, adjusted her name tag, then asked Jasmine again, "What did you order Miss?"

"I ordered two salmon and rice dinners," she continued to smile.

"Oh, I am so sorry! I completely got distracted…Marsha Allah, we're out of salmon…"

Jasmine's reaction was so nonchalant that I wanted to tell the waitress off for her…but knew better…this wasn't the time to make a bad impression. I kept quiet. "No salmon. That's fine," Jasmine said, "What else do you have?"

"Yes," Rasheeda relaxed a bit, "Cod, and I'm sure we have some whiting."

"Ahh, let me think," she answered as though she wasn't sure.

"I'll come right back. Would you care for a complimentary drink for all the inconvenience?"

We both asked for iced tea. Jasmine's was ordered unsweetened. We finally had a chance to talk. "Sister, I know we just met but would you consider having dinner with me?"

She took a sip of tea, swallowed hard then said, "I have to pick up my daughter."

Oh God, I thought to myself, she's married…I should have known that. "I…I didn't mean to impose my Queen, ah, it was selfish to not even think before I asked."

She almost chuckled, "I'm picking my daughter up from my neighbor. My husband and I have divorced."

I was relieved and curious at the same time. Most Muslims stay married.

Our waitress interrupted, "Thank you for being so patient…it's my first day."

"That's fine," Jasmine set her at ease, "I'll have the whiting…with rice and cabbage." I was enjoying her company. I didn't feel the need to fill in the silence.

"I haven't seen you around before," she finally asked me, "So, where are you from?"

"All the way from Cerritos. Cerritos, California."

"I'm from California too…Brentwood."

"Al-hamdullilah. Allah took us halfway across the country to meet in this small town." We both found that to be pretty amazing.

"Brentwood, huh. That's exclusive property."

"It's my stepfather's house."

The restaurant was gettin' pretty noisy. Tables being set. People talkin' louder. Waitresses laughing and serving orders.

"Nice," I smiled admiring her beautiful hands. "I'm here working construction."

She listened, and I went on to say, "I'm not married. I have a son…lives in Los Angeles with his mother."

Her voice almost forceful, "This is the holy month, your family should be with you."

"Well sister, my ex is not Muslimah…nor is my family… God is still working on me."

The sound of the plastic bags rustled as the waitress handed our dinners to me. I had to speak up this time. "Sister Rasheeda, you brought my dinner to go?"

"Oh, I thought you were together," the waitress apologized.

The waitress and Jasmine seemed to be giggling. So, I laughed too. It's corny, but I felt I'd always known Jazz. I had that haven't-we-met-someplace-before look written all over my face. At the time, I convinced myself that we were simply two Muslims going through the Holy month. As for me, I knew I was doing the best I could to get back on the right path, the "Musta-quim."

She walked pretty fast, so I had to step it up to escort her through the busy crowd, then opened the restaurant door, and motioned my hand for her to pass in front of me. The air was filled with the sweet aroma from the restaurant. My stomach growled. "Sister Jasmine, may I walk you to your car?"

"Thank you."

"Such a clear night," I smiled, eyeing the moon illuminating the sky above us.

"Yes," she responded, "It is a very beautiful night, praise God."

A family walked briskly past us engaged in jovial conversation. "This night is special...you probably won't believe me, but my parents met in a restaurant...not in a Muslim restaurant. But it was still a restaurant."

"Yea, I don't believe you," she laughed.

"I didn't think you would...it does sound like I just made it up, huh?"

"How old are you?" she asked, "If you don't mind me asking?"

"I'm almost twenty-one."

"Oh," she said sounding startled and instinctively she backed away from me.

"I'm not that young, I'm a parent...just like you."

I opened her car door. Jasmine gently turned the ignition key. The battery whimpered, she smiled, turned it again, this time it whined. She quickly pressed the button to pop the hood, rolled up her sleeves and exited the car and started checking the engine. Two steps in front of me I followed her then I said, "Okay my Queen, let me try to start it."

Jasmine ignored my request and asked me, "Do you have any jumping cables?"

I tried to start it with cables but it was more than a problem with her battery. She wouldn't ask for a ride home, so I insisted. I realized on day one that this woman can definitely hold her own. After I drove her home I went back home, showered, and went to sleep. Early the next morning I told my uncle what happened and I arranged to have Jasmine's car towed to the shop.

"Transmission, around $2100 to fix it," the mechanic sighed, "I can cut the labor in half for you."

"She's by herself and she can't afford to spare that kind of money," I shook my head. Just then another tow truck was backing in the lot preparing to set down another car.

"Young man, you can leave the car, I'll work around it, let me know."

I knew right then I couldn't call Jasmine with that kind of news. I went home to Uncle Joey instead. "She doesn't have that kind of money. I don't know what to do." He was just starting to polish off the wax on auntie's Cadillac.

"Well what do you want to do?" Uncle Joey asked me candidly, positioning the cloth in his hands.

I thought long and hard, and calmly said, "I want to marry her."

Uncle Joey stopped and gave me a stern look. "I'll loan you the money to fix her car, but you pay me back before you get hitched."

"I can do that," I said smiling.

"Curtis," he grinned, "Congratulations!"

"I haven't asked her yet."

"Sounds like you will."

I knew what I wanted. But I wasn't even sure if Jasmine would have me. Maybe she was more accustomed to millionaires with expensive cars wearing business suits. She seemed so independent. Maybe she wasn't even looking for a man.

I woke up a little early to my make sure my hair cut looked clean and wavy. Showered. Prayed. Dabbed on a hint of my best cologne. Then I got the ironing board out and put a fresh crease in my work pants.

ALTHEA JEWEL

FIVE

It was Monday. I was so nervous that I almost stumbled as I opened the car door for Jasmine and her five -year-old daughter, Maryam.

I liked her daughter's name. It was Biblical for "Mary" Mother of Jesus.

Maryam peered up at me from the back seat. "Do I know you?"

"My name is Kareem, nice to meet you!"

I gave Jasmine a quick glance and then she explained, "Maryam, I told you last night that the car is broken and Mr. Muhammad will be taking us to school for a short while."

Maryam was a beautiful chocolate brown skinned girl. She was wearing a school uniform and her saddle oxford shoes were scuffed and worn. Her oversized vest covered a crisp white blouse with rolled up sleeves. She was a chubby kid and her clothing made her appearance seem even larger than she actually was. Her dark brown hair was just above her shoulders, neatly pulled back in a ponytail.

She was a soft-spoken yet boldly honest, like most kids. First, she repeated her mother, "Mister?"

It took me by surprise and then she added, "Excuse me Mama, but is he old enough to be a mister?" It was odd for a child this age to be so outspoken, but in all fairness, I was a complete stranger.

"My name is Kareem, nice to meet you and you can call me Kareem, I'm not Mr. yet," I chuckled. I adjusted the FM radio, to a song that was a classic 1970's Memory Lane, by Minnie Riperton. I thought I was in line to sing along, "I stumbled on this photograph, kind of made me laugh," until they both made fun of me.

"What?" I stopped singing and asked them, "You don't like my singing?"

"You are singing?" Jasmine giggled.

"Okay Sister Jasmine, you can do any better, let's hear it."

Jasmine closed her eyes momentarily, concentratin' like she was holdin' a microphone, and sang in perfect harmony followed by an octave high enough to almost shake the dashboard. Wow, and Minnie would have been proud to hear another sister with such quality range. Yep, I nodded, this is the woman for me. That song, in those few minutes, unfolded our keepsakes, and magnified our collective memory lanes.

"Al-Hamdullilah," I smiled, "Sister, your voice is beyond beautiful."

I glanced back at young Maryam, who for the moment had settled into her own comfort zone. I made a quick stop at the neighborhood coffee shop, leaving the keys in the ignition. "You ladies wait and I will be right back."

"Maryam, do you like orange juice?"

She nodded yes. I came back to the car and gave the small pink box of pastries to Jasmine, then carefully reached to the middle of the back seat and handed the juice to her daughter.

Maryam hesitated before she said, "Thank you."

"You didn't have to do this," Jasmine added, implying that I was fussing over, or spoiling her. Maryam kept silent watch studying how I reacted to her mother's comment.

I kept quiet until I pulled up to the student drop curb, "Okay ladies....This is your Captain speaking please remove your seat belts and exit the aircraft to your right," we all laughed.

"Mr. Kareem!" she shouted at me before taking her mother's hand to walk away, "School is out at 12:45, I'll be here five minutes after the bell rings."

"Ask your mother it's whatever she says."

She and Jasmine whispered a few sentences and then responded, "Mama says okay!"

Jasmine answered, "We'll be standing right here at 12:50 at the latest 12:55."

"Okay, I will be waiting for you right here, at 12:45 this afternoon."

Later that week I was talking to my aunt about my new love interest and her phone rang. "Yes, who is this?"

Auntie muffled the receiver and asked me if I wanted to talk to Traci. "Ah, he's not here, is everything okay?"

I walked towards the refrigerator, grabbed a picture of ice water then sat back down at the table. A few seconds later she said goodbye and I asked, "What did she say?"

"She wanted your new pager number. I told her to ask you, not me."

I sipped the water, burped, "Excuse me," then walked back towards the pantry.

"Traci knows not to call here anymore…period," I grabbed a box of raisins and closed the door.

A few days later, Traci called back. My aunt expected her to call again.

"Listen here, you calling here is just disrespectful."

She continued, "What do I mean disrespectful? My nephew is getting his life together, even after you tried to mess it up!" I can only imagine what Traci said to get this type of reaction.

"Are all you Whitfield girls even taught to act like you're respectable?"

Aww damn…that was fierce. After a few more colorful words, my aunt calmly hung up the phone. "Curtis," she said, "I'm sorry, I had to set that gal straight."

It was 1984. Aaron was two-years-old. I was home in Atlanta planning to try to visit him. But first, I wanted to let Jasmine know of my plans. I headed over to her apartment. Parked outside. Climbed the stairs, popped my jacket collar, and raised the handle on the door knocker. I gave it two solid knocks, paused and tapped it three more times then waited. That was our passcode so she'd know it was me outside.

Jasmine greeted me with that energy and her gorgeous smile. I got a quick smooch before Maryam burst into the front room…holding a book. "Brother Kareem!!"

Maryam's big smile and a hug, made me feel at home.

"As-Salaam-Alaikum. And how is my African princess doing today?"

"I'm just fine, thank you," she said, "I am learning Arabic now."

"Tell me what you've learned."

"Today is Sunday, that's Ahad in Arabic."

I could hear the water runnin' from the kitchen and smell the sweet spices cookin'. Maryam continued to recite the days of the week and relished my approval. As she set the book down, I noticed she was wearing the bracelet I gave her. "Ah, I see you like the bracelet."

She shyly nodded yes.

Last week, to hear Jazz tell it, she was showing off her jewelry at school and had to be scolded. I didn't see the harm in the child expressing she was proud of her belongings. But it wasn't my place so I just kept quiet.

Jasmine entered the room without wearing her hijab. It took me by surprise. I coaxed her to sit for a moment between us. Her daughter politely excused herself. "You're doing good with her Jasmine."

She leaned back extended her arms and stretched, "Thank you Kareem."

"I hope I can be a good parent someday." After I announced my hopes for parenting it got awkward. I broke the silence and went real old school on her, "Whatcha cookin good lookin?" Pops used to say that to Ma all the time.

Jazz answered giggling, "Broiled salmon with spinach and mashed potatoes."

Good meal. Good company. And it's all good. She chopped up some onions, garlic and some fresh basil for the fish then served up her homemade chicken soup as an entrée. I said a short blessing. I'm telling you, this woman had my heart in her hand. For real. Jasmine washed and I dried the dishes while I told her about my plans to visit Los Angeles.

"Allison won't bring him here," I said bluntly.

"A son needs his father," she said softly.

I placed the last bowl in the cabinet and Jazz took the dish towel from my hand.

"You just have to believe in yourself," she said reassuringly, "Allah knows your heart."

I didn't even have to explain it to her. She already knew me. For a long time, I thought that all women wanted was for a man to be some type of superhero. Well, the one's with daddy issues typically do. But she was different. Jasmine understood that sometimes a man just needs to know that somebody's got his back, while he's getting stronger for the both of them. It was already after 8pm. We were still comfortable, so I hadn't worn out my welcome yet. Jazz parted Maryam's hair and combed it out, then neatly braided each section. Twenty minutes later, her daughter gathered up the hair supplies, kissed her mother, and said goodnight before going to bed.

"Thank you for a perfect night Jasmine but I should be going."

"Kareem it's still early," she smiled, "Unless you have somewhere else to be."

"Nowhere I'd rather be than right here." I could hear the wind rustling through the tree outside. I reached over and pulled the awning, slowly closing the window. These old Atlanta buildings had a special charm. I understood why people moved from bigger cities and settled down. Yea, I was going to be comfortable here too. Insha Allah.

Unmarried Muslims, and probably something similar in other religions, were supposed to be escorted and definitely not alone together in the same house. I admit, I knew we were not doing the right thing by seeing each other so intimately. Even if we weren't having sex. The fact that we were both grown, and sexually attracted to each other, was pushing the envelope. But I knew I wasn't going to take advantage of her. She was a mother, a Muslim mother, and I respected that. We drank hot cocoa and watched some TV show…I couldn't tell you anything about the show because I was only paying attention to how she made me feel, just by being around her.

At home, she didn't wear her "hijab" hair covering. She wore her hair in twists, short and curly, perfectly sectioned and very attractive. I touched her curls, smoothing them down around her temples.

"God you're pretty!" I smiled and she shyly responded, "Why do you always say that?"

"Can't a brother tell you the truth…girl you are awesome."

I was hopin' for her to just come out and say it, but she didn't, so I asked, "Where is your ex?"

Her natural calm voice changed abruptly, "Back on the island with his wife and kids."

That caught me off-guard. "Back on the island, what do you mean Jasmine?"

"Kareem, I don't want to mislead you, but it's complicated."
She took a long pause, "He was always married, just not to me."

I know that most women have their lives mapped out in
their minds. They think by a certain age they should be at
a certain place. At a certain milestone they need to achieve
what they imagined. But real life doesn't work that way. We all
get side tracked. Detoured. Off-course. She told me she met
Maryam's father when she went by herself, on vacation, in
Jamaica. By the way, just to put things in context, she wasn't
Muslimah then.

She didn't sugar coat it or play the victim. "I was just caught
up and we didn't use any protection." Wow. She's honest. She
didn't have to elaborate on that because I'd been there before.
Several times. "And when I told him I was pregnant he tried to
say that maybe it wasn't even his baby."

Oldest line in the book. Irresponsible asshole taking
advantage of somebody. Probably still makin' that move
somewhere today. Leave his wife and kids at home. I pictured
him like I imagined my grandpa…on the beach, always
stepping over another shell.

Jasmine's head was tilted, she looked up towards the
ceiling. After not blinkin' for almost a minute, I realized she
was trying to control her tears from falling. It seemed like the
right time to come clean with her about my history. I didn't
want her feeling like once again, a man withheld his truth, his
life from her without putting all the cards on the table.

"Jazz I want you to know something," I said in a solemn
voice. "I made two mistakes with my baby's mother. Well, at

least two that I know of. The first, was moving here without knowing if the relationship would last long distance."

By now I had her full attention. "Why do you live so far apart?"

"I asked her the same thing," I laughed. "She wanted me to stay in California and work anywhere, even if it was for minimum wage...but I wanted something better, for me, for her, for my son." Jasmine set down her cup and waited patiently for me to tell her the rest of my story.

"I sent for her a couple months before the baby was due. And, ah, I thought she was coming...and when I went to pick her up from the airport...her sister shows up with some big lie and I was stupid enough to fall for it. I guess, all along I'd told myself I wasn't good enough for Alee...and her sister, in a twisted way, closed a door that was never really opened."

I didn't go through every detail but I did tell what the outcome was...I'd slept with my girlfriend's sister. Jasmine called it the "sabotage break up" when you think it's impossible, so you subconsciously do something so terrible and it destroys the relationship, forever. After going to see Jasmine for a completely different discussion. It sorta changed direction. But you know what? I was relieved to get the truth about Allison's sister out in the open. I went home that night and slept soundly knowing there weren't any skeletons or secrets between me and my future wife.

"Congratulations Curtis!!"

"Thank you," I responded, "But Uncle Joey worked this out. I can't take any credit, yet." It wasn't my plan to own any property yet. My plan was to get financially strong and now

I'm spending money before I can make enough of it. My uncle taught me everything he knew about the construction business. I got my license and I learned the basics from foundation to roof. After three short years I earned my first degree…home ownership.

SIX

Pops surprised me with a gift of $20,000 to buy new furniture and appliances. "That's too much money," I said quickly.

"You don't want to be settling in on credit," Uncle Joey slapped his hand on my shoulder. The house closed escrow a day before my birthday on April 14th.

"Curtis, should we toast your birthday?" Auntie smiled, holding up a champagne glass.

"Shit, that's right, the day we pay taxes, I should remember that!" Uncle chimed in.

"Yea, my lucky day!" I raised my glass, "Cheers!"

Even though they understood that as a Muslim, birthdays and Christmas weren't celebrated. And though I didn't expect gifts, I had done so growing up in a Christian household. To be honest, I didn't miss the annual make a fuss over me every year for one day...and possibly mistreat me at least a few times the rest of the year. That's not necessarily Islamic, that's just me.

That summer was extra special. Once or twice a week we'd finish up early at the job site and take a detour to check out my new property. Uncle Joey was just as excited as I was when we got there. We drove up to the curb and admired the steps leadin' up to the front door. It was a beautiful sight. The rooms facing the street had really nice windows and shutters that gave it a real pop. I would imagine myself, coming home with Jasmine and Maryam, and seeing the proud looks on all our faces. This was going to be the place we'd call home.

By sunset, we watched the sky change colors to a blend of orange and pink. It looked like summertime in Las Vegas. "Uncle J, look up at that sky!"

"Pretty huh?" he said, wiping the sweat from his brow.

"Yeah, that color reminds me of those pink bird feathers in Vegas, what do they call that bird?"

"Curtis, we got no time to be daydreamin' about Tequila Sunrise at the Flamingo Hotel in Vegas."

My hands were so calloused that the sweat wouldn't fill up the creases, but I was happy. For the first time in my life, I felt like I knew where I was goin'. A few days later, I got up the nerve to move forward.

"Will you be my wife?"

Jasmine sounded a little hesitant. It was a big step though. "Are we ready?"

"I've been ready since day one," I said as I leaned in closer. I was thinkin', if we're not ready now…when will we be.

"Day one?" she kept smilin', "That sounds so sweet…ready since then?"

I hesitated before I said, "Come on Jazz, we're not gettin' any younger." That was our ongoing joke we're not gettin' any younger, when either of us wanted to have our way.

She grinned, "I'm not…but Kareem, you have plenty of time."

I looked away for a minute, thinkin' what to say next. "Don't you love me?"

She didn't hesitate, "Yes," she whispered, "I do love you."

First, I gave her a long unreligious kiss. Her lips were so soft. Then, I opened the tiny velvet box. I remember thinkin' I was supposed to give her the ring first, and then kiss her…but I guess I got that part a little mixed-up.

The ring, Ma's first ring, a plain gold wedding band but it has been in the family. I'd kept it. Waitin' for the right time. The right girl. "We can go pick out another ring that you like better, if you want to," I added.

She started to cry, "It's perfect!"

I believed we started out right. No secrets. No surprises. Now that it's official, let's get right down to business. Since both of us are from California, we should probably get married, or rather, celebrate there with family. She agreed.

"Momma, is Brother Kareem my daddy now?"

"No, your father lives in Jamaica." Someday we'd cross that bridge.

Maryam forced her weight on her mother's lap, hugging her neck. "Momma, you're getting married?"

Jasmine held her daughter close smiling, "Yes my sweet, we talked about this."

"Yes, and…"

"And?" Jasmine asked then said, "Come on Maryam what do you want to ask me?"

Just above a whisper she asked, "But why can't I call Brother Kareem daddy too?" We were both stunned.

"Or is he just my step dad?" she asked with uncertainty.

Jasmine was not sure what to say, "Some families do call... ah...but."

I interrupted, "Maryam, I'll be doing everything I can for you and your mom...from now on."

"Oh, she said, "Well, that means it's settled. I'll just call you my dad, from now on."

We spent some time figuring out where to have a Muslim wedding ceremony. Jasmine was happy to mention there would be no traditional white dress, or walking down the aisle throwing a bouquet. We went to the courthouse and got our marriage license on Tuesday, August 14, 1984. The next day myself, Jazz, and Maryam, drove to California for the best part, our celebration.

"Salaams Brother Kareem!"

"Salaams Ahmad, As Salaam Alaikum!"

Mrs. Muhammad's orange hydrangea and white flowers lined the walkway to the door. I loved the concrete pavement, completely new, then touched the Arabic insignia door knocker. I rang the doorbell and Ahmad opened the door.

"Salaams, Brother Ahmad," Jasmine greeted him with a modest gaze.

"Ah, you are more beautiful than my brother informed me," Ahmad said. He hugged my wife.

"No hand shaking, we are family now!"

"Watch him Jazz, he's crafty with the women!"

Mrs. Muhammad, originally from Saudi, entered the foyer, wearing a turquoise dress and her gold jewelry. She extended a youthful hand to greet Jasmine and then reached up to hug me. "Al-Hamdulliah!"

An hour or so later we'd finished unpacking. Mrs. Muhammad, Jasmine, and Maryam enjoyed "sweet cakes" and tea while Ahmad and I got busy settin' up for the tomorrow's wedding celebration.

"I thought you would never get over that Whitfield girl," Ahmad laughed.

The neighbor's dog started barking at a cat cruising over the top of Ahmad's back fence. "When did you get a cat?"

"Brother, that's not our pet...it just likes to tease the dog."

Ahmad had put on a few pounds. He was 5'10 and I just made it to 6 ft. For years I thought I was going to be shorter than him. Now I'm the tall skinny one. "You know, her sister just popped up over here the other day."

"Who, Traci?"

"Yes. I was pretty shocked to see her too."

"We were organizing the tables, the side gate was open, she walked back like she owned the place."

"No shit, what did you tell her?"

"I told her that you were getting married to a real woman, a down home Southern girl!"

Ahmad's gaze followed me, "What did I say wrong, my brother?"

"She's from Brentwood."

"No shit?" I detected a little champagne and caviar in her walk, hahahaha."

"Yea, she does walk like a queen...but she's from out here."

"Are your parents coming?"

"We'll see...they've been invited."

Ma wasn't sure that a Muslim wedding was right for a Christian family. What she didn't understand was that being

Muslim doesn't mean I don't cherish the values I was taught. And though I was given a Muslim first name, only those close to me called me Kareem. I would always be Curtis Morris, son of Wesley and Claudia.

"Come on, help me set up, want a beer?"

"Beer?" I chuckled, "You got anything stronger than that?"

"Brother you're not allowed to get cold feet."

"No, I'm fine, where's the good stuff?"

A few minutes later, Ahmad handed me a shot glass of Johnny Walker Red. "I'm glad you're Americanized, my brother, I sure needed a drink."

Mrs. Muhammad broke up our short party and gave us instructions to sweep the sidewalk down with the water hose. Later, Ahmad's father's clean Mercedes pulled up on the curb and parked in the driveway. Mr. Muhammad was an accountant for a large manufacturing company in downtown Los Angeles. His business shirt had lost its crispness from the day. He moved slowly from the car, and breathed out 5:30 afternoon 10 East Freeway stress, still gave me a cheerful, "Curtis! My son! Look at you!"

"Let's have a toast!" we touched shot glasses. "Enjoy tonight," he whispered, "You won't get another good night's rest again in your life!"

My body froze and then he tapped me on the back and laughed, "Just kidding."

Jasmine and Maryam slept in one of the two guest rooms. I was in the other. Early before sunrise, I squinted my eyes and found my way to the adjoining bathroom. A few moments later, Ahmad and I scurried to prepare ourselves for the day ahead.

"It's prayer time, my brother." We stood side by side as Ahmad called the "Adhan" the Muslim call to prayer. I remembered thinkin' how strong I felt that morning. Like nothing could touch me or bring any harm to me or the people around me. We all take it for granted. Not everything good is promised to us. And for a brief moment, I had forgotten that no matter how on top of the world I thought I was, it's just another snapshot in time.

Later that afternoon, I realized somethin' else. The same peacefulness I'd felt in Georgia, I was feelin' today. I had bought a cool black suit to wear after the ceremony, case anybody thought I couldn't. But I wore a traditional Muslim outfit for the wedding. It was so comfortable I never changed into my suit. I felt like an African king. But Jasmine stopped the show with her gown. It was a beautiful shade of coral, a color that complimented her brown skin tone. And she picked a dress that showed off her lovely curves. I was so proud to see her dare to not be too modest. It was a change that I'd hoped would become routine.

There were less than a dozen guests, all that I considered family, and our ceremony lead by Imam Suleiman, honestly, the people that mattered most in our lives.

"I bear witness that Muhammad is the true and righteous messenger of Allah, Peace be upon him." After the entire Shahada was recited, the Imam blessed our union, and then we exchanged rings. Shahada is similar to when Christians are born again and accept Christ. Every Muslim must accept the religion at the onset. And again, during times of renewal. We both renewed our promise to each other and to God.

"Curtis," Jasmine grinned," I want you to meet my parents. Mr. & Mrs. Goldstein."

Now don't get me wrong, coming from California myself, I've interacted with many creeds and nationalities. But she never mentioned her mom remarried a white guy, a Jewish white guy. We were in the foyer taking more photos, I extended my hand to him, "Pleasure to meet you sir."

Lawrence Goldstein, must've been early 60's with a firm handshake and a distinctive gap in his teeth. "Excellent wedding…and as you can see, beauty runs in the family, this is my wife, Priscilla."

I held my peace. This guy sounds entitled. Like he's bragging on marrying a Black woman…like that made him more of something or please notice me, I'm cool now. Jazz embraced her mother and greeted her step dad. It was short and sweet. Hmmm guess she's not completely on board with this cat either.

Jasmine's dress flowed as she and her mother walked away. I caught the corner of Goldstein's eye watching my wife walking. Beauty does run in the family but you better keep your eyes on your own wife…stop looking so hard at mine.

He turned back around, "So, I hear you and Jazz are practicing Muslims."

"That's right," I smiled, making eye-to-eye contact.

"Is your family Muslim?"

He began fidgeting with one of his cufflinks. Looking down and looking back up at me. "You know," I said without blinking, "There's a whole lot of talk about the differences between Islam, Judaism…and Christianity."

Still trying to fasten it, he said, "Yes but how so?" I leaned in about a half a foot and helped him button the cufflink, then put the palm of my hand on his arm and held it there.

"It's not the differences Mr. Goldstein," I stated, "It's what we have in common that's much more important."

He nodded without saying anything. And I released his arm and said, "We all want the same thing. But until we own up to our similarities and stop exploiting our differences… nothing's going to change."

I waited a moment for him to process that thought. "Yes, that is true. What…what did you say you do for a living?"

Now he's sizing me up. "I'm a contractor, Dr. Goldstein, I'm into real estate development." If you could have seen that joker's face. Him being a cardiologist and all. I wanted to make sure, damn sure, that we don't underestimate each other.

Mr. Muhammad intervened, "Hello. I'm Sam Muhammad, Ahmad's father."

"Nice to meet you, Lawrence Goldstein," they shook hands, "Lovely wedding, and you can call me LG." LG? He's been chopping it up with a couple of Muslims and now we're on more cool mode.

Mr. Muhammad didn't stutter, "Ahh, Mr. Goldstein, yes, well there's a room for you to hang up your coat, if you like… and to your left, the dining room, please have something to eat."

Goldstein walked towards the house and Mr. Muhammad said, "Didn't I warn you?"

"About what?"

"After marriage not getting another good night's sleep!"

"Naw man you said you were just kidding."

"Kidding? No, just didn't want to scare you off."

We chuckled a minute or two. I finally answered, "I think I can handle it."

Jasmine's step father, Goldstein, was a character. He moved to Brentwood for the short commute to his office. He met Jasmine's mom when she was on the rebound from splittin' up with Jasmine's father. Marrying her when it wasn't popular to his religious peers but Priscilla wasn't shacking up. Not with her fourteen-year-old-daughter. Jazz never liked him. Not because he was white. He made her feel like she was in a white dollhouse on display.

Six months later, we moved into our new home in Atlanta. Maryam started first grade. Jazz and I were on a health kick. Which, by the way, was the best move I could possibly have made. I made toast while the blender was mixing my morning health drink. Life was good. "Maryam, close that refrigerator all the way, please."

That's right. Let these kids know electricity isn't growin' on trees. And nothing else. Every day around 5pm, home from work, I changed clothes and went for a three-mile jog. I missed running. If I was being honest, even though it's been some years, I was still broken up over Waleena. I don't think I'll ever get over losing her. But you know, we find comfort in doing what our loved ones did when they were with us. If they liked baseball we play or watch games and remember the good times. Running gave me somethin' to hold on to. A piece of her that made me stronger.

Even with everything going smooth, it had been over a year since I'd seen my son. A lot of cats would call that shameful. Yes, I felt ashamed. Up to now, I kept my mouth shut and sent Allison money every month like I was "supposed to" as Ma put it.

I whispered to my wife, "This is killing me."

She nudged me, "Do you think it's a good time to try again?"

Alee and I had argued constantly now that I was married... and I heard she flipped when she found out about the house that I'd bought. Long ago, I imagined buying one for her. Part of me understood how she felt that way. Another woman, with another child, was benefitting by being with me, not her. But why do women, who had the choice to be with a man, choose not to be with him...and then get pissed off when he's doin' better with somebody else?

"Go upstairs Maryam. I need a towel and the blow dryer, okay?"

"Okay Mama."

I was goin' over the plans for my next project and poured another tall glass of juice. Jasmine hugged me tight, "I have something to tell you."

"Yeah babe, I ahh..."

"Jazz, just tell me!" I was just about to read the morning paper when she got my attention.

She whispered, "I missed my period." I stood dazed for a split-second, then picked her up and spun her around, my shoes squeaked on the kitchen tile.

"Relax," she laughed, "I won't know anything until I see the doctor, next week."

I was already suspicious that something was different about her…"I knew it!"

Maryam skipped into the room, singing a hopscotch rhyme, and handed her mother the towel. "Maryam, enough already, that song is getting on my nerves."

"Come on now, what's wrong with that?" I smiled, "She's happy let her sing her song."

Even before I knew for sure that Jasmine was pregnant, I stopped letting her do a lot around the house. It was funny to see me with a soapy bucket of water cleaning up. I don't like to do "water sports" as I called it. Not all water. I'll wash dishes, as Ma said, they don't wash themselves…And I don't mind doing laundry. I can fold and fluff better than a military baby. But I was known to run away from sponges saturated with Comet. And mops in buckets scented with Pine Sol.

In the beginning, Jasmine was everything that I ever hoped for…and more. She didn't care if we didn't have a dime. She had my back and I knew it. I wasn't losing any sleep. Not one bit.

"Kareem, sweetie," she handed me the phone, "It's someone named Marvin, he needs to talk to you."

"Hello."

"Brother Kareem, As Salaam Alaikum!"

I sat up in bed, "Marvin Whitfield?"

"I've been asking about you and folks lips are tight…man how is life treatin' a Brother?"

Jasmine eased out from under me, her feet gently touched the floor beneath the bed and she disappeared down the hallway. "We're all doing fine. It's chilly down here compared to L.A."

"Righteous. Same old same old out here," he chuckled.

"Have you seen Alee?"

"No, I heard she's back in school getting her business degree or something."

"Yea, that's nice. I haven't seen Alee in two-and-a-half years."

"No shit?"

"No," I said sadly, "I saw my son the day after he was born... haven't seen him since." Marvin was a decent cat. I visualized all of us back when I lived in Cerritos.

"I'm sorry to hear that," he responded in a solemn tone.

"So, what's going on?" I finally asked him.

"You know, Curtis me and you we're cool. I don't believe anything I hear. And you know, they talk plenty shit...but I never bite my tongue so most my peeps turned their backs on me."

I kept silent and he continued. "I know I got issues...but I can't find a decent job down here. I don't want to mess it up and end up in jail again...I need to get away from L.A."

I changed ears on the phone, then asked him, "You not on parole anymore, right?"

"Right, since last year."

By now I've pushed all the covers off and I'm sittin' up in my bed rubbin' my goatee nervously.

"I know you are workin' construction and I've done a little of that I'm pretty handy," he added. Handy? I don't think he could even change a flat.

Jasmine handed me a glass of water, I sipped it…slowly. "Curtis, are you there?"

"Yeah, my brother, I'm here."

I thought to myself. I repeated his words in my head: I don't want to mess it up and end up in jail again. "Where are your kids?" I asked, drinking more water.

"They're fine. They with Cookie, she got a decent job."

"They don't respect me, Curtis I just want to make this shit right…"

I took a big gulp of water, "They don't respect me much down there either."

Jasmine nudged me for a time out. "Curtis, can we talk about this," she whispered. That was my husband cue. We need to agree on somethin' before I CAN decide.

"Brother Marvin. My uncle is the boss. I'll call him in the mornin' and call you back." I handed the phone back to Jasmine and she gently placed it back on the receiver.

"Whatever you decide, just sleep on it," she said softly.

I remembered that night. I did more pacing than sleeping. My wife woke up feeling refreshed. "So?" she said yawning.

"I think we should give him a chance…so I can get back to havin' my rest again."

Jasmine worked to get the house ready for Marvin's arrival. After cleaning the upstairs, she went down to the guest room and aired it out. She seemed excited about meeting someone from the Whitfield family, even if it was the black sheep.

"I felt like I had nowhere to go, when my mom married my step dad, I know what he's going through."

I just kept an open mind, "We'll see," I said, then ran the vacuum cleaner through the front hallway. After my evening jog, I drove to the Greyhound bus terminal to pick up Cousin Marvin. It was a long wait. Maybe we should have pieced the money together and sent him an airline ticket. Just as I was beginning to lose hope, I saw him. He was even thinner than I remembered. At 25, he appeared to be much older. His hair was graying and his face was ashen, he was terribly dehydrated.

I offered him a hand with his worn luggage bag. "Let me help you with that," I said extending my hand.

He tossed the heavy black bag into the cab of my truck with one hand and said, "I got it."

"You know," he said nonchalantly, "I'm little but I got the heart of a gunslinger!"

I shook his hand and patted his shoulder firmly, "Good seeing you again!" We stopped on the way and bought some household items: laundry soap, toilet paper, milk, eggs, and some Jolly Rancher candy for Maryam.

An hour later we got back home. "This is Jasmine, my wife."

"Ah ha, congratulations, baby due too!" he said smiling.

"Hello. It's very nice to meet you too."

ALTHEA JEWEL

SEVEN

As a gesture of Southern hospitality, I offered to show Marvin around. Took him sightseeing. First, we drove to see The Skyline, the tallest skyscraper in Atlanta. It starts downtown and continues north through Midtown. In Midtown, we looked at The Bell South building and watched a beautiful sunset and panoramic view of the city.

"Righteous! Thank you for showing me the town, now where are the honeys?" I had forgotten his player attitude. I changed the subject telling him we had a lot of work to do.

"Never mind the honeys brother, let's get this money," I joked unapologetically.

Uncle Joey wasn't playing either, "Curtis, you ready for this?"

"Yeah, Marvin has all his tools and I'm showing him the city so its time, what's next?"

"Corporate Towers Center is starting next week," Joey said firmly. The contract was going to be for one of the tallest suburban buildings in the entire country. I told Marvin this is a big project. All he had to do was follow instructions. Everything would be just fine.

Looking back, it's perfectly clear that he hadn't been payin' attention from the beginning. But I said it anyway, "Starting Monday, we'll have breakfast, then head out to work at 5:00 am."

On day one, I tried to keep it simple. Walked the site and explained what the job was. Handed him a check list and some tools. Uncle J and the other workers did most of the heavy lifting. "Are we coming back here every night?" he complained.

"Not every night. We don't want to waste time back-and-forth...get a motel room and lay over."

"Okay, sounds good," he said reluctantly. I knew by the way he responded that Marvin was not cut out for hard work. This was going to be a tough job and I did not want or need to be babysittin' a grown ass man.

"So whatcha think?"

"I don't know," Uncle Joey scratched his head...but give him credit he ain't struck out yet."

My uncle was always the patient one. He reminded me that it takes time to learn any craft. I just wanted this project to work out so we'd have future business to count on.

"Wow," Marvin said, gawking at his first paycheck.

Uncle Joey and I were checking the figures for the inventory and supplies we needed. "Marvin, I need to explain how the accounting side of this works."

"I see how it works!" he laughed out loud, "Damn! This money is sweet!"

Marvin started out contributing. To the household. And sending money home to his wife in California. Well, they weren't married but he'd been with her so long it was pretty much common law. A month later I was asking myself, what the hell was I thinking? Marvin barely knew what he was doing and wanted to supervise the workers at the site. That was daytime. Then after work, he was bossing Jasmine around in my four thousand square foot home.

"Marvin, telephone," Jasmine yelled to him from upstairs.

"Sister Jasmine, can you take a message and I'll call them right back."

I spent a whole lot of time in my back yard. My grass got cut more than the lawn at the White House.

"Curtis, Marvin needs to get it together, or he has got to go!" Uncle Joey finally caved.

"Okay, I'll see what I can do."

Jasmine and I had been married for a year with no problems. Today we had words, confusion, sounded like an argument. She left the room almost in tears and I realized that my wife was feeling the strain of being so close to havin' a baby along with our house guest. It had worn her down.

A few days later I stopped by Uncle Joey's house. "How's it going Rain?"

"Curtis! Look at you, growing a beard."

"You like it?"

She walked up close and touched my face, "Not bad." I kissed her cheek and then sat down at my favorite spot in the kitchen.

"How long has your company been here?"

"Couple months."

She set a hot bowl of homemade chili in front of me. "Left over corn bread?"

"Yes ma'am."

The steam from my bowl swirled up, in front of me, like dancing smoke signals. "How's your wife holding up?"

I stirred my food and blew gently as the steam settled. "Baby's due soon, she's restless."

My uncle had been working on his truck. He washed up in the adjoining room's laundry sink, running a good force with the water. Auntie handed him a towel and sat down next to us. "Man, I hear Marvin is even showin' out at church!"

I usually keep my cool when Uncle J teases me but this was a sensitive subject. "Yea, maybe I should rough him up a little."

"No son, don't start doin' anything like that." Uncle Joey bowed his head at the table and blessed his food, then started eating.

"I think you got pulled into some of that Daddy Whitfield guilt." I hadn't heard that in a long while. My mother used to speak on that.

Later that day Jasmine thumbed through a catalog lookin' for baby nursery furniture. "I was thinking," I said, then sat on the bed next to her. "He's puttin' a strain on our family and I won't let that continue, you know?"

"Curtis, I'm sorry for yelling at you the other day."

"Yea, I know...you're under enough pressure right now... we all are."

Jasmine set the book down and put her hand on top of mine. "I was working on the budget and lost a receipt."

She pointed to a white bassinet and matching dresser and I listened while she flipped to another page. She got my full attention when she said, "I found this empty pill bottle in the kitchen trash bin."

The long pause gave me a minute to understand where she was going with all this. "What? When did this happen? And why didn't you tell me?"

"I was prayin' there was a logical explanation and I don't like starting mess."

I just gave her a curious look…Miss Nosey diggin' in our trash cans findin' prescription bottles. I just laughed. She held onto the bottle. "He's taking prescription drugs."

"Let me see that."

"RX# 452371 Marvin Whitfield …Vicodin. Take twice daily as needed for pain…500 milligrams each."

"Where's Marvin?"

"In the den," she went on to say, "Watching or being watched by the television."

I never even discussed it with him. What would a pill head say about takin' pills? I just wanted him out of my house. Away from my family. I bought Marvin a ticket back to California and he left without questioning me. A plane ticket, so he would land much quicker and hopefully he'd get some help.

"Cookie, yea baby it's me, Marvin, I'm coming home."

ALTHEA JEWEL

EIGHT

"AAAAHHHH!"

"That's it, PUSH!"

Halimah Morris was born, July 23, 1986. Weighed just under eight pounds and was twenty-one inches long. She came into this world a perfect "10"

And this time, I thought to myself, I am where I am supposed to be. By her side. "My queen, you are amazing!" I couldn't say anything else. Jasmine too exhausted to speak, simply nodded and smiled back at me. My wife and I didn't agree on her name but now, she was Halimah. Halimah is a Muslim name, it means "humane" or one with humility. Historically, Halimah was the nurse who raised the Prophet Muhammad. Peace Be upon Him.

"She's absolutely beautiful!" I held her firmly those first few moments and thanked Allah for entrusting me with charge of her life. I kissed Jasmine. Told her how much I loved her.

"Jazz, now don't you start boohooing. Be strong like your daughter, be strong." Dr. Bahtia, our obstetrician, coached us through the delivery and the critical after birth which I watched in sheer agony and amazement. I know that nowadays, people video tape the whole birth…that's a little too much for me. But I did get one of the nurses to take a snapshot of me, proud papa in scrubs holdin' the baby. They discharged Jasmine on the 25th and we returned home to decorations, balloons, flowers, and gifts set up by Aunt Lorraine and Uncle Joey.

"Welcome home Halimah!"

"Mama!" Maryam was anxious to be closer to the baby and her mom.

Our baby daughter, slept soundly in Aunt Lorraine's arm with Maryam a breath away. "She's somethin' special Curtis," Aunt Lorraine exclaimed.

"You know who she looks like?" Uncle Joey added, "Waleena."

At that moment, I recalled the baby pictures of my late sister. It was a pleasant memory. I smiled, "Yea, you're right, she sure does," I laughed.

Every four hours, the feedin' the diaper changin'…man, what had we gotten ourselves into?

But I was grateful. I thanked Allah for my blessings. I was twenty-three-years-old and I didn't ever want to do anything to mess this up. Not this time.

"Cousin Marvin called to check on things with the baby," Jazz announced. Marvin had returned to Los Angeles with a new outlook on life. He was studying to get a contractor's license and moved to Rancho California (later known as Temecula). It was a fresh start for him, Cookie, and their four kids. He never told Allison or Uncle Bernie that he'd even been to my house in Atlanta. That bothered Jazz. She wanted to let them know we had compassion for family, when they had not. It wasn't that I didn't agree with her. But I knew in my heart that tellin' the Whitfields that I was nice to someone in the family didn't absolve me. As long as I lived in Georgia, I was still an absent father in their eyes.

Speaking of which, a few months later, Jasmine decided she wasn't fulfilling her life's dreams. "Maybe I should start thinkin' bout going back to work."

"Why?" I thought she wanted to stay home a couple years with the baby.

"I don't want to lose my skills." Jasmine said anxiously.

This girl had a master's degree and was overqualified for every job she'd ever had. "Okay, so we'll find a babysitter so you can go back to work."

"But I'm just saying…I want to go back, but not right now."

I peered up at her from my newspaper, flushed the toilet and said, "Then don't go back yet." She closed the bathroom door and I finished up, washed my hands and opened the window to let some air in.

"Jazz, I think we need some fun time off, you want to go to the movies?"

"What? You're asking me like we're still teenagers," she chuckled.

"We don't have time for a date."

I set the nails in place to hang a new wall fixture. Afterwards, I placed my arms around her waist, whisperin', "We can make time." The way I saw it, she was doing a lot. She kept my house and my children. She was always buying the girls "something" and rarely spent time or money on herself.

She once told me that she felt "guilty" if she even thought of doing things like she used to, made her feel selfish. However, two more long months of silence passed between me and my wife.

"What's wrong babe?"

"Nothing Kareem."

"Don't say nothin'...it's obviously something." She had cut off her curly locks off and practically shaved her head. As beautiful as she still is, I missed those golden reddish curls she'd always adorned, until now.

"Why did you cut off your locks??" The bathroom was filled with steam and her perfumed body lotion fragrance lingered in the air.

Jasmine mumbled somethin' under her breath and faced me, "I just wanted a change."

Her tone was defiant and controlled. I stood alone in the foyer a very long minute. "Okay Jazz, I'm going out...into the city...for a while." My patience was runnin' out and I was frustrated...nothin' I said made it right. The chill in the air outside almost cooled me down as I mashed the gas pedal and drove off. I needed a peaceful distraction. That southern peacefulness. Up where we live, houses are more spread out, to preserve the landscaping. But five miles or so closer to the city, there were new house developments sprouting up all over the place. Some I had built. I felt blessed.

I chuckled to myself that if Jazz and I were having troubles, this is the best place to live should our disagreements turn into arguments. And if our arguments got out of control, nobody could even hear any yelling or God forbid, dishes breaking on the kitchen floor. But I was hopin' to prevent all that by this gesture of peace…and I hope that this time I'm right. "How much you want for him?"

"250.00, she's first generation…pure."

"I have two children, one is newborn…will she get along at my house?"

The man at the pet store smiled, "Oh, they're the best protection and family dogs." As I was petting my new dog, the other Lab, a brown one…wagged her tail and let out a pitched yelp. "She's high-strung…pretty color, looks like chocolate brown, but I don't know," he chuckled.

"I'll take her too." I bought a few basic supplies and some dog chow and gently packed them in a blanketed milk cart, in the passenger seat of my truck. They slept the whole way.

"TWO dogs…Curtis?" She called me Curtis, with a tone, when she was upset with me.

"Yea, I went to buy just one, I couldn't leave her sister there…I had to buy both of them."

Just in time to break up the argument, eight-year-old Maryam came to my rescue. "Oh, Mama, they're so cute!!"

"Yea, can they stay?" I winked my eye at Jazz. She was breastfeeding, smirked, then started laughing. Maryam couldn't leave the pups alone. They got more attention than the baby. If we let her, she would fall asleep right next to them.

After about a week she announced both dogs had names: "Data" was a mocha-brown with green eyes, and "Stormy" was jet black. Data was not as high-strung as the pet shop owner told me. She just needed a home and a place where she could grow. I promised Jasmine that when the weather warmed up Stormy and Data would be moving outside.

"You might need to move out back with them," my uncle laughed. Shit, I thought to myself, Uncle J didn't know how close to the truth he really was. From my large bay bedroom window, I enjoyed the back drop of eucalyptus trees growing in rows in the distance. My property was huge. In fact, I could have built another house on the lot but I treasured the openness of nature.

All too suddenly, I opened another window to the sound of electric saws and hammering on the soon-to-be completed house at the end of my almost empty street. "We'll be having some company soon," I smirked.

"Yea, I saw the wife over there a few days ago."

"Oh, really?"

"Uh, huh, she's a real nice white lady."

"Oh really," "I asked, "They got any kids?"

"I don't know…it was just her and their housekeeper."

Atlanta was already getting Hollywood, I laughed, "Uh oh, there goes the neighborhood."

That's what some people say about my people…I was just tryin' out the terminology in reverse. It still didn't feel or sound right. I was glad another family would be moving in. "Maybe they have some kids to be friends with Maryam."

Jasmine pinned on Halimah's cloth diaper and kissed the baby, "Maybe."

I had a break in the construction work. And decided to use the time to get my house painted and renovate my bathrooms. First, I would attend to the master bedroom. I needed to dress up the balcony. I wanted to give my wife a peaceful space where she could relax and enjoy the view from upstairs. It felt like a lifetime ago, when Jasmine and I spent time together, downstairs by the fireplace when Halimah was almost two months old. We were closer. I prayed we could get back to paying each other a little more attention. Just the simple gestures even, although a man has his needs too. I wasn't asking for too much. Or was I?

"Can you watch the baby while I take my shower?" Already five months old. My goodness! I kissed her forehead, reinforcing my baby talk.

"Pea pie Pea pie...picky- picky- Po'- pie."

The rest of 1986 zoomed by. On January 2, 1987, a huge moving van pulled up slowly with an out of state license plate. The Johansen family was making a grand entrance. I was in my front yard and turned the sprinkling system off and waved. He in turn, waved back.

Maryam was allowed to play outside and ride her bike, if she didn't have a lot of homework. Since she was not going to a Muslim school, she would not wear a hijab. Only when we went to services. If we had been from another country it might have been different. Besides that, Jazz was pretty strict about the rules. Only ride on this side of the street. And under no circumstances was she to leave the block. One time Jazz couldn't see her from the front porch and put the girl on punishment for over a week.

Must've been a few days after the new neighbors moved in before Maryam met our new neighbor's son, his name was Lenny. Nine-year-old "Lenny Jr." was a skinny kid with slicked back, sandy colored hair. He was almost my daughter's height.

The dogs were restless and I took them out with me for a quick jog. "Hi neighbor!" I extended my free hand to Mr. Johansen.

"Why hello, I'm Lenny."

"I'm Curtis Morris. Wanted to let you all settle in before coming down to meet you." Data was ready to keep moving, she shook her tail frantically.

He chuckled, "Nice dogs!!"

"Yeah, thanks, well you let me know if you need anything. My house is the one…"

He cut me off, "Oh yeah, are you workin' over at that big house?" he pointed to my property. He went on to say, "They must keep you busy, that's the biggest house, so far, on the block."

I almost chuckled, "Yea, that's my house, I don't work there. Me and my wife moved in…couple years ago."

He patted Stormy on the head, "Oh, my apologies…how absurd of me…"

"Ha," I laughed out loud, "No problem, you probably saw me in my work clothes. My wife always renovating. Gotta keep the Mrs. happy." And with that out of the way I noticed him looking at me a lot different. I jogged in place and tightened the dog's leashes pullin' them closer towards me.

"Well, I guess you got your hands full," he joked, "Nice meeting you Curtis."

"Nice meetin' you too, Lenny." That interaction would be one of many for me in my neighborhood as time went by. When I was younger, I thought it was because I was younger. But as I got older, I realized it was just how assumptions without facts, really goes. I knew for a fact that Alee wasn't the type of parent to introduce our son to society's reality. Since she lived in her own world. And if I wasn't careful, Aaron would grow up in that bubble and not be prepared for manhood. Oh yea, there's preparation involved. My parents did their part as best as they could. But to be honest, it was my uncle that showed me how to be responsible. It was my friend Ahmad that introduced me to being disciplined. There was so much more to becoming a man. And it isn't just physical... it's emotional too. And once you become, then it's just as important to navigate it properly. Or there won't be many benefits.

"Hello."

"Alee, it's me Curtis," I paused to give her time to respond, praying for her to hear me out. She went on talkin' bout random stuff. I sensed she was just nervous. It's awkward talkin' to someone you don't get along with when you haven't spoken in a while.

I finally asked her, "Alee, how are you doing?"

"Good, Curtis, everybody is ah...well, just great, how are you?"

"Good. I've been trying to call you, is everything okay?"

She could hear Maryam and the baby playing in the background. I walked into the den, sat down on the sofa for a little privacy. I guess I was a little nervous too. I just decided to leap in, "I apologize for not calling you before now. There's really no excuse. But I'm in a new house. I'm hoping we can get on the same page about Aaron now. It's been four years." I was hoping to reclaim my time...at least some of it.

"My cousin Marvin was defending you at the 4th of July picnic."

"Yea, what did he say?"

"That you put him up in your house for a while and set him straight."

"Naw…didn't set nobody straight. He just found out there's a right and wrong way to do things."

"Well thank you, he seems to be doing better now."

I tried to not steer too far away from the reason of my call. "Listen. I know last time we spoke you were workin' and going to school and we talked about Aaron and you coming to visit. Anyway, I just finished gettin' my house together and I was wondering if now is a good time…you know, for you to come out here…"

I could hear little Aaron in the background asking her, "Mom, who's that?" He never did call her Ma, mama, or mommy, it was always mom. My boy was educated.

A few months later she finally gave in. "Okay, but I can afford my own tickets."

"Say hello," she handed Aaron the phone. But she didn't intro me as his father. As soon as Aaron said hello she took the phone from him.

"Bye Curtis." She hung up. I kept holdin' the phone in my hand until the dial tone sounded off.

"Are you okay?" Jasmine asked, handing me a plate.

"That was Alee, she's finally gonna bring Aaron out here to see us." She did that thing where she looks up at the ceiling to hold back the tears. After dinner, I showered, prayed, and kept to myself for the rest of the evening. It was a lot to process.

And thankfully Jazz gave me some space. We prepared for Aaron and Allison's visit. Up to now, I had been sleepin' in the spare room. I shuffled my comforter and pillows, not back upstairs, but to the den.

She asked me the next morning, "Why are you keeping your things downstairs?" Was that a trick question? Had she forgotten we haven't made love in almost six months? But I'm not in the mood today. So, I didn't answer. I just stacked up my bedding, neatly. Halimah is just barely walking…she wobbles then holds onto the chair for support.

"Kareem, I wish you wouldn't ignore me like that…I just asked a simple question."

"Jazz, we have guest coming in less than a week…let's fix up the spare room."

She eased up on the conversation, "I'm going shopping later, you coming?"

"Sure," I shrugged my shoulders, "I need some things."

Thinkin' back, I must have lost my mind. I filled the freezer with seafood, steaks, and lamb chops. I polished furniture and bought some paint to spruce up the guest room.

"Curtis, how much are you going to spend?" In the back of my mind, I wanted my son to be moving in, permanently. I planned to pick up Allison but she rented a car and drove in from the airport.

Aaron peered out the back window of a clean Lincoln sedan. He reminded me of a million-dollar-star-child… spending a week in the countryside to see how the "other-half" lives. Alee popped the door locks and I reached to help her with the luggage bags.

"Aaron!" I hugged him. No resistance, I picked him up and hugged him again.

Allison's eyes scanned the landscape and scenery outside and seemed taken by surprise. "Wow, this is some place you have here!"

I smiled modestly, "It's been a long time, looking good, nice rent-a-car too."

"You like it. Ah, this is all that was left," she added, "It's so big I can barely drive it."

"Go on inside, me and Little Man will bring the luggage in, right Aaron?" Aaron was never shy. He just stood there, taking it all in, waiting to make his move. I handed him the smallest bag, "This one's heavy can you carry it inside for me?"

He scrunched up his face and unzipped his jacket, then said, "Sure, this is easy."

Allison had matured. She swore she'd gained ten pounds…I didn't see it. I guess it had been a while but Alee had managed to cheat time…she looked younger.

"My name is Aaron," he said with confidence.

"I'm so glad to meet you! I'm Jasmine," she smiled, "How old are you?"

"Five," he answered and the baby babbled her talk.

"And this is Halimah."

He smiled and touched the baby's hand then asked, "When is her birthday?"

Jazz grinned, "July 23rd."

"My birthday is March eleventh," Aaron proudly announced.

"How was your flight?" Jasmine asked, getting a feel for her new guest.

Alee nodded, then said, "Just fine, I want to thank you for letting us stay here, we could have…"

"Could have nothing, we don't let family stay anywhere but home." I chuckled to myself. Even though Jasmine had put me out of my bedroom…she always had real good manners with company.

"Where is your other daughter?"

"Maryam's in Brentwood, California…visiting her grandmother. My mom flew down and they left early this morning." My rich father-in-law loved spending money on those turnaround trips. But this time it was pretty good timing since Aaron was comin' and I didn't know how it would turn out. Maryam loved her grandfolks. They spoiled her. I guess that's okay every once in a while.

Jasmine's flower garden had finally bloomed. I remembered thinking she was spending too much time on it. Today, the entry way looked impressive. "What kind of plants are those?"

"Velvet Boxwood," Jasmine said, "The roses in front of them just bloomed."

Alee nodded, "Lovely."

A bluebird rested above on a tree branch, Data barked, and Stormy wagged her tail. It was all of sixty seconds but Allison held the baby. Halimah's pacifier fell out as she watched Allison and then pushed away wanting to be on her own. The baby was fascinated by Aaron. He let her press her tiny hands on the side of his face and smiled.

We played with the children and Alee went to freshen up. Thirty minutes later Alee entered the room wearin' her signature tight T-shirt and a pair of jeans. She'd taken off her traveling hat and pulled her hair back in a teenage bun. The style brought life to her freckles and Cherokee cheekbones.

She sat down next to Aaron and he caught her attention. He hugged her, "Mom, I'm hungry."

"Okay, but first you need to get cleaned up…"

I stood up and clapped my hands twice, real loud for emphasis on getting it done. "Your mother's right. Get out of those airport clothes, get comfortable."

"Okay," he said reluctantly, "Curtis you wait right here!"

"I'll wait," I smiled and Allison laughed. We stayed up pretty late that first night. We played board games, watched old movies and ate a lot of junk food. I was getting all those years of waiting out of my system in one night. Aaron and I fell asleep in the den on the floor with a couple of blankets and pillows between us.

The next morning, Jasmine came downstairs and woke me up, requesting diapers. "Okay Jazz, I'll go buy some." Jasmine was a little bit edgy about Aaron and Alee visiting. I guess she didn't expect us to get along so well after all…it had been a long time. To be honest, it shocked me too. Everybody thought it was going to be such a disaster. But so far, we hadn't stirred up a storm much less a hurricane.

I came back with a surprise from the store. "What's all this?" I handed Jasmine a bouquet of spring flowers and a couple bags of Pampers, kissed her cheek and headed straight through the patio doors.

"Aaron, you like camping?"

He said no but Allison reminded him, "Remember you went with Grandpa?"

Aaron stretched and yawned, "Oh, yea," he scratched his head, "That was a long time ago."

The phone rang once, twice, three times before I finally picked up. "Kareem!"

"Ahmad?"

"As-Salaam-Alaikum!"

"Wa-Alaikum-As-Salaam, Ahmad, man where have you been?"

"I just started working at Cal State…teaching again."

"That's good, we need to make that bread to eat!"

"You are so right, so what's going on my brother?"

"Funny you should call today." I gave the phone to Aaron. He carried on a conversation as though he knew Ahmad. I almost fell out laughing at how grown up he is. He politely said goodbye and went back outside near the patio to play.

ALTHEA JEWEL

NINE

"He's here with Alee. They're staying a week."

"Man, she finally is coming around! Allah is merciful."

"Yes Sir. That's a fact…Ahmad when you coming out here?" I went on to say, "Maybe we can meet halfway, you know, I'm workin'…I love bread too!"

"Ha! Ha! That's for real." Aaron came back inside the house as Jasmine's voice rang out from upstairs. Something about taking Allison shopping today…and see some of the town?

Ahmad paused, then asked, "How's the new baby?"

"Just fine, she's taking a nap." By now, I've been ready to get off the phone and Aaron was getting restless. He wanted me off the phone too. Kids sure do come in handy, I grinned.

"Okay Brother, I'll talk to you later." After I hung up Aaron rested on the carpet and set puzzle pieces for Arizona, Colorado and Texas, right on the money and looked up at me for a nod of approval. I lounged on the sofa with my head resting on a pillow…that lasted all of five minutes.

Aaron couldn't hold it back any longer. "She called you Kareem. I thought your name is Curtis."

"Well, I was born with the name Curtis. But I'm Muslim, my religious name is Kareem." Jasmine handed me the mail, slightly opened the blinds, and exited the room, humming.

"What does that mean?"

"It's okay, everybody doesn't have one."

"Aaron, come over here…have a seat, sit down, next to me."

"It's kind of like a middle name," I finally said.

"What's a middle name for?"

"Do you know who I am?" I asked almost half serious.

"Yes."

"Who am I?"

My young son answered quickly, "You're Curtis, my mom's friend."

My mom's friend, was simply put, my soul felt like someone had tossed it into a trash bin. "That's right, I'm, I'm a…a… friend."

He studied my expression then asked, "Curtis you're married?"

"Yes," I snapped out of it, stumbling for the words, "Jasmine is my wife."

"Oh, that's right," he said sounding disappointed. I was too rattled to speak so I just listened. "I told my mom she needs to get married…and you seem like a real nice guy."

"Oh really, you so sure I'm a nice guy?" I laughed managing to make a silly face. He teasingly slapped me and I tickled his neck and his sides. He laughed so hard he got the hiccups.

Halimah let out her attention yell. "The baby!" he shouted and bolted towards the stairway.

"Aaron, stop running!" Allison chimed in from the guest room.

"How could she hear you running, the door is closed?"

"Be quiet," he whispered. "Mom has rabbit ears."

Even the dimple in his chin deepened as mine does when I breathe quietly. When he turned to the side, our profiles, almost identical. I wished I hadn't stayed away so long. You hear people say, dad, mom, why were you gone so long? And that person was me now. I hated myself for who I was. But I didn't know how to change it.

A few hours later keys jingled as Jasmine and Allison returned home giggling…door closing and top lock turning as I rose from a cat nap. Both ladies were taking off their shoes and placing them on the rack. They were actually enjoying each other's company.

"You like barbeque?"

"Yes," Aaron said with enthusiasm.

"Tomorrow I'm going to show you how, okay?"

"Okay."

The next day I showed Aaron how we men can work together in the kitchen and prepare a good meal…on our own. The sweet smell of salmon croquettes and fried potatoes was impressive. Alee still wearing her pajamas sat down at the kitchen table. "You need any help?"

Young Aaron immediately asked her, "Mom, why aren't you dressed?"

Suddenly all the attention was focused on her outfit. A tight pair of cut off white lounge pants showed off every curve in her body. She was also sporting a loose fitting tank top exposing a tattoo on her upper arm? At first view I was merely glancing at the tattoo. I looked twice. And then, looked a third time…it was the same Egyptian circle that I had on my arm. Aaron was watching my reaction to what must have been a conversation between the two of them and I was just a sidebar.

I held back my laugh, "Alee want some tea or coffee?"

"Coffee," she smiled and then winked, "I feel like drinking it black."

She never drank black coffee. I guessed she was lettin' me know that I didn't know her anymore. I didn't think too much about it…besides that haircut and copycat tattoo she was still Allison Whitfield. By day three, I got comfortable and let my guard down. Nothing could go wrong. Not with my world… finally my prayers had been answered, at least I was beginning to think so.

Stormy barked playfully at me when I started setting up the tent in the back yard. I was gettin' a bit annoyed with her; my reaction was my first warning and I rationalized it, ignoring the sign. "Move Stormy!" I kept movin', "You're in the way!!" Stormy stopped the fuss and put her tail between her legs, then lay resting at the edge of the lawn. Data was occupied in their doggie home chewing on her plastic bone and keeping a watchful eye on our house guests.

Aaron named it The Big Green Ball it was a real camping tent that slept four adults with no problem. The plan was for Aaron and Alee; me and Jasmine (alternating with the baby) to sleep the whole night "under the stars"…then Jasmine came down with the flu and that changed everything.

"Aaron, you want to roast some marshmallows?"

He scrunched his nose at me and asked, "Won't that burn them?"

Aaron Whitfield, my son, nothing but laughs. Earlier, the weatherman had hinted of rain. It wasn't to be. Not tonight. Not a cloud in the sky. Just a big beautiful moon and a million glistening stars above us. For more than an hour, all three of us were like children, time suspended in the adoration of God's creation. The sky above us, the earth beneath us, and the air between us was in complete harmony. Aaron rested his head on my shoulder and Allison lay in close proximity next to me.

"I see why you moved here, it's so beautiful."

"Yeah, it's pretty cool." Aaron was beginning to get sleepy but fighting it all the way.

"My little Man had a long day."

"You've certainly kept him busy...he's going to sleep like a baby."

"I'll be back I need to check on Jazz and Halimah." I was tired when I went back inside through the sliding glass door and up the stairs. When I reached the bedroom, Jasmine walked into the adjoining bathroom and closed the door. I took a peek behind the curtains. The tent was directly below our bedroom facing the other direction. I heard the toilet flush and then the sound of water running through the sink. It stopped. She cleared her throat and gently pushed the door between us opening it until it creaked. My wife stood for a moment before the nightstand and leaned over, to set her alarm clock. Her faded nightgown suddenly cast a shadow, not a silhouette, on our bedroom wall. I'd asked her once before why she kept it…she insisted it was snuggly and comfortable… and just a gown, to sleep in.

"Allison's a pretty young woman," she said without making eye contact. It felt as though Jasmine had been readin' my mind. I kept silent as she tied down her hair with a brown satin scarf.

"Jazz, thank you so much for being in my corner with all this," I leaned over to kiss her.

She pushed me away and turned her head. "Stop, I don't want you to get sick too."

"Look, Jazz, whatever is going on between us we need to fix it."

"I don't know what you're talking about?"

"This. Me sleepin' in the den every night since the baby came home."

Her face dropped. "Can we talk about it later?"

"Yeah, I guess so…after Aaron goes back to California?"

In a much sweeter tone she asked, "Can I say something?"

"Yea."

"What's the story with Aaron not calling you Daddy?"

My eyes blinked a few times, then I said, "He doesn't know I'm his father." Her expression said it all. This was worse than either of us imagined. I had been banished with no passport. How could I possibly return?

She finally said, "That's messed up." And she added, "She is going to make him suffer to spite you."

There was a light tap-tap-tap on our bedroom door, then Aaron's voice, "Curtis?"

"Yes, Aaron, you may come in." Aaron pushed the door slightly and walked to the edge of the bed and sat down next to me. "Aaron, are you having a good time?"

He nodded his head yes. "Curtis, are you coming back outside?"

"Okay partner, let's get back to our campsite."

"Goodnight Jasmine, I hope you feel better."

Jasmine appreciated my son's thoughtful gesture. "I'll be better after I get some rest."

I touched Jasmine's arm reassuring her that everything's alright. "You want me to get you some juice or anything?"

"No Curtis, I'll be just fine...leave the door open so I can listen out for the baby."

Aaron and I stayed up until almost midnight while Allison slept in her sleeping bag. Finally, the house and the yard campsite were quiet and I contemplated going back inside. "You're not leaving me back here in the woods, are you?" Allison whispered.

"No, I..."

She sat up and looked over at Aaron who was sleeping, snoring actually. "Does he snore like that all the time?"

"No," she laughed, "Just when he's really tired."

"I'm tired too...we did a lot today. I could use some sleep."

"Alee."

"Yes."

"I want you to know how much this means to me."

She tilted her head towards me, "I know."

"I don't want you to take this the wrong way...but I'm glad in one way and sad in another."

"Why are you sad Curtis?"

"I'm sad because you are never going to accept me for who I am."

She moved in close and calmly said, "I've done an excellent job pretending…doing everything to get over us…but I…." I felt the hairs on the back of my neck rise up.

"Pretending?" I felt my eyes water and I blinked hard to make them stop.

Then she began to cry. "My God Curtis, what do you think I'm talking about?"

"I don't know Alee, but I need to know why?" I stopped before I said anything else.

"Need to know why?" she blinked her eyes at me, "Why?"

"I was praying we could get back on the right track…" I stammered.

"Go on and say what's on your mind…Curtis."

"Why doesn't Aaron know that I'm his father?"

She shifted her weight away from me, she misunderstood me, again. "You did it…not me!!!" she shot back boldly. I went straight past her accusation and blurted out, "But he's my flesh and blood Alee, he is my son!!"

If hindsight is 20-20, then add forty more. It was as though I never even heard the words you did it not me…I went straight to the stable, let the horses out and didn't bother closing the gate behind me. I kept talking, "You've never given me a chance." The stampede was inevitable.

"Curtis, you ruined it not me. You slept with MY SISTER so don't tell me about giving you a chance!!" she cried out, "I wish you weren't his FATHER!!"

Aaron was no longer snoring but still asleep, tugged at his covers to distract us, momentarily. "Oh no Alee, it wasn't like that!"

"Are you telling me you didn't do it??"

The tent felt like a helium balloon ready to pop. I felt sick to my stomach the way I did that morning after…with Traci. I left the tent and ran towards an empty space on my lawn and hurled. After I stopped throwing up, I washed off my face with the garden hose. Even the dogs wouldn't come near me. Alee was on her way back inside the house, with Aaron in her arms still asleep. I dropped my hands in defeat. She slammed the sliding glass door so loud that it echoed across the hill and vibrated back in my head like a boomerang.

I barely slept that night. The next mornin', I stared out the patio window at The Big Green Empty tent. The only good thing about it was that it couldn't laugh at me for being such a jerk. The sliding glass door had a big crack in it. Allison Whitfield had left her mark in Atlanta. I took my place back on the den sofa. I heard Jazz say something to Halimah. I got up and made my coffee. When my wife came into the kitchen, I was still eyeballing the cracked glass on the sliding door.

"What are you going to do?" Jasmine said abruptly.

I couldn't pretend. I knew what that meant. It was my responsibility to fix this mess that I'd made. "I can't do anything…it's already been done."

An hour later, Allison came out of the guest room and asked if she could talk to me in private. "I've decided to cut our trip short."

I was expecting that. "Okay," I said in a low tone.

She explained it. "I thought if I came here and we got a chance to talk about it, face to face, somehow everything would work out."

"It feels like you came all this way to confront me…not to finally get me and Aaron together."

"You're asking a lot of me Curtis."

"Alee, I know I hurt you. I was wrong and I should have told you but I was ashamed…not one day went by where I didn't think about telling you. But she set me up. Told me you were sleeping with some red head white boy while you were pregnant. I was wrong…dead wrong…but I can't undo it."

"What am I supposed to do now?" she said with tears flooding her eyes.

I didn't have an answer. She waited half a second, then shook her head and continued packing her luggage bags. That was it. I asked myself the same question what am I supposed to do now? As I closed the guest room door behind me, I thought about Jasmine's question…What are you going to do?

It wasn't just the cracked glass or even The Big Green Tent that she was concerned about. Jasmine hinted and Alee confirmed this whole thing. The fence was back around me. There was rust on the lock but the barbed wire was still intact. She was never going to forgive me. I just had to accept that. Jasmine called a friend at the car rental office and asked for an overdue favor.

"Remember the teacher's aide from work, Miss Woodbridge?"

"Uh huh," I said without really listening.

"I know you're not paying attention to me. I think we should take Allison and Aaron to the airport."

"How? They drove here." I said…still not wanting to hear her.

Jasmine was already preparing…the baby was dressed and she was almost ready herself. "We can drop her off and take the rental back to Miss Woodbridge," she said softly. Jasmine brushed her hair back for a few more minutes and pinned it up in a high bun. The front was already curled in a bang. She wisped her hand securing the new style and winked back at me in the mirrored reflection.

For a moment I was back on the right page. "Sounds good, so how do we get back home?"

"Miss Woodbridge's husband works at Hertz…by the airport. That's where Alee rented the car."

"I don't know. Everything is so messed up."

"We shouldn't let her drive back, not leaving here so upset." I was numb. I tried to come up with something to say but no words came out. I wanted to talk to Aaron but I decided he was too young to even understand… I'm sure his mother let him know they would be leaving today. On their way…back to LAX a million miles away from me. I put on my best poker face and together we watched an episode of The Flintstones. Aaron did all the laughing.

"I have something for you Aaron." I took the roll of film from my Kodak camera and placed a new roll inside, then handed it firmly in Aaron's right hand. The camera was almost bigger than him. I showed him what to do to take basic photographs.

"Ask your mother to show you more…she used to take pretty good pictures."

"What do you say Aaron?" his mother said softly.

"Thank you." He looked proudly up at me, reinforcing his appreciation. "I will take good care of your camera."

"It's your camera now," I said smiling, "I know you'll take very good care of it."

It was time to get going. I buckled young Halimah in her car seat. Jasmine was standing next to me holding the diaper bag. Allison decided to place Aaron in the passenger front seat, buckled his seat belt and closed his door. I remembered how I felt, like we were going to a funeral. I felt a slight burn in my stomach. I watched Alee get situated in the back seat behind her son, her body language, hollow, disengaged. I had planned to drive, but I ended up asking Jasmine, "You feel like drivin'?"

I handed her the car keys, she moved up to the driver's seat without saying one word. I sat in her seat, in the back, with the baby between Alee and me like a divider between us. Jasmine adjusted her seat, and drove on, periodically looked in the rear view at the baby and me. Mind you, there wasn't any fancy navigation system in any cars yet. Just good old sense of direction and if necessary, a Thomas Guide. Aaron paid careful attention to the road and enjoyed his conversation with my wife. Other than that, the ride was completely silent. Jasmine maneuvered that Lincoln like it was her own.

Halimah napped and I looked straight ahead. Allison fidgeted, sniffled and dabbed her eyes while still wearin' her large framed sunglasses on a day when the sun decided not to shine. "Call and let us know you made it safely," I managed to say at curbside.

Alee had regained some of her composure, removed her sunglasses and said, "Okay."

Her slanted eyes were puffy. Her face was flush. She was pretty, even at her worst. The porter was gathering their luggage bags and Aaron stood patiently waitin' to say another goodbye.

"Young man, Aaron, it was so good seeing you," I lifted him, held him, kissed him and he giggled as he squeezed the back of my shirt collar with his tiny hands, hugging me back. My eyes were red, I could feel them watering up, but I pushed that feeling down deep inside. Told myself, I must be strong.

"Come on Alee give me a hug?" I held my hand out to her and she gave it almost against her will. It ended up being a brother and sister embrace. A long one. Probably would be our last.

"The doctor said I have heartburn."

"What?" Aunt Lorraine sounded surprised.

"Yea, I have to ease up on spicy foods and take pills if it gets any worse."

"When did he tell you that?" I continued removin' the headboard on the bed in the guest room and laid it against the wall.

"Last week."

"How's the family?"

"Maryam's back from the west coast. Aaron and Alee left last week, and Halimah is flushing toilets all day."

"We were prayin' she'd let him stay here with you for a while."

"No, no chance of that happening."

"Have you heard back since they left?"

I felt that familiar burn in my chest again, "No...not yet."

After I gave the tent away, I replaced the broken sliding glass door with a better one. I signed up to be an assistant coach at the local youth basketball camp. At night, I relaxed out back on the patio deck. I started smoking a pipe. The cherry and mahogany fragrance floated past my backyard before sunset. I called Ma. "Hey Ma, how's everything?"

"Fine son, I was just thinking about you."

"Oh, I'm alright. I'm doing better, no more stomach pain."

"That's good news. Listen, Lorraine just called me. Curtis, you can't change the way people think."

I guess Auntie told her about Allison's disastrous visit. "Nope," I said solemnly.

She reminded me, "Children are…"

I interrupted, "I know, Ma, children are a blessing from God…they belong to Him, not us …"

That was late Friday evening. I hung up the phone and wondered, why me? Ironically, the next day I received a letter from Allison, I stood outside at the mailbox and opened it, then began to read it.

May 3, 1987
Dear Curtis:
I am sorry that I haven't been in contact with you like I promised. Thank you for giving me some space to figure things out for myself. I have to admit, I didn't give you the credit you deserved when we were together. I realized that when I came to visit you in Atlanta. I cannot say that this is forever but for now, it is too painful for me to do this back-and-forth

communication between you and I, even if it's for the sake of our son. I will wait until he's a little older. I don't want him or me to be in the middle anymore. I live here and you're doing well in Georgia. I just learned that you came to see me the day Aaron was born. I apologize for doubting you. I wish with all my heart that I could forget that Traci and you ever happened. I thought I could forget you and forgive her. But one more piece of me dies, every time I see her face. I wish I was fearless and strong just like you. I wish I could find someone to love me just as I am. Jasmine truly loves you. I can see that you got it right this time.

Respectfully,
Allison Whitfield

I was still standing motionless on my front driveway. The mail carrier was delivering more mail across the street and said hello, I waved back and sort of frowned as I placed her confirmation back inside its envelope.

That night was the first night that Jasmine and I made love again. It was better this time. I guess we both had been through enough to learn how to forgive. We wouldn't forget. But for now, maybe we could find ourselves back in the picture again…and for once be proud of being there.

"Come, before the sunrise, let's pray together." We both showered and afterwards I called the "Adhan" and recited "Al-Fatiha." My wife never mentioned nor did I ask about our drought that lasted so long. I did show her the letter. She read it…then placed it back on the mahogany dresser without saying a word.

"What do you feel like doing today my Queen?"

She flashed her dimpled smile and said, "I wish we could go back to bed…"

I kissed her earlobe and whispered, "Yea, I could make love to you all day."

Just as I put my arms around Jasmine's waist Maryam walked into room with the baby. "Mama, her diaper is wet."

"So?" I spoke up and waited for someone to respond.

Maryam stood in her tracks, holding Halimah with one hand and said, "I don't know how to change her." This was a teaching moment. We'd just transitioned from cloth to disposable diapers. I grabbed a wipe and a Pamper with one hand and Maryam's free hand, then led her towards the nursery. From then on, it was pretty much routine. Maryam was given chores to do on a daily basis. Nothing too physically challenging but she did learn to change her little sister's diaper. Unless it was a stinky.

Maryam spent her allowance money on very interesting, extraordinary things for a girl her age. Her interests ranged from telescopes to soccer balls and practically anything in between.

"Maryam, you ready?"

"Be right down!"

"Okay, I'll be out in the car…practice in ten minutes." We played about five miles away at the middle school gymnasium. I had to get permission to have the parking lot open to the team and any parents that wanted to watch their kids practice and play on the weekends. The court was 50 50. An old floor with no shine to it and a manual score keeper, who I had to recruit weekly. But at least there was some interest in the game.

As coach, I found a way to stay in shape, keep up with the community, and introduce my daughter Maryam, to team sports. There was one catch: The only kids that signed up to play basketball were boys, not girls. The following Saturday morning, a group of them gathered at 10:00 for orientation and registration.

Maryam sat quietly, right next to me, observing and listening to all my instructions. "They don't look ready to me," she said on the way back home.

I scratched my head and laughed, "How do you know?"

"You can't switch your pivot foot while handling the ball."

"You're right…. Absolutely."

We lost our first game. It was a blow out. 50 to 32. It wasn't just mechanics. We just didn't have the rhythm and didn't play well as a team. One of the parents gave me a stare hard enough to make my hat fly off but I didn't flinch. After I explained where we went wrong and scheduled an extra practice day, we made it back home.

Halimah screamed like somebody was beatin' her brains out. Jasmine kept combing her hair. "I mean, I'm the coach!! They totally disregarded the plays and seemed afraid to try."

"How old are these boys?"

"The oldest is twelve."

"Why do you put all that pressure on yourself…it's the first game?"

"Jazz, they need more than coaching," I said sadly.

"Maybe you should just put Maryam in."

"No, not yet…more ground to cover before we can make

that move." The baby settled down and Jasmine wiped the tears from her reddened face. "Halimah, look see how pretty you are?" I showed off her reflection in the mirror.

Jasmine put away the extra rubber bands, comb and brush and hoisted the baby on her hip. She followed up with another question. "What is Maryam doing in the meantime?"

"She's my assistant," I beamed proudly.

It was pretty obvious. She really only does the warm up… and after that she's watchin' everybody else play. Maryam was patient. The boys were not as disciplined as she was. But we kept workin' at it. Bobby Hauser, Spike Jones, Carlton Richardson, our neighbor's kid Lenny Jr, Otis Smiley, Clarence "CC" Pierson, and the Cochran twins…received their basketball uniforms with pride.

"Wow, this is going to be a great season!" The first hurdle was getting everyone to meet for practice, on time. Clarence, our tallest and most talented player was notoriously late. Sometimes he didn't even show up to practice. He waltzed in halfway through our next game.

"Sorry Coach, it won't happen again…" I stopped him in his tracks, "Sit out Pierson."

I'd benched him and his dad took it personal. He was a sports advocate but he was also a blabbermouth. When I was lenient on his son everything was kosher. But after I benched "his boy" he gave me body language like he was going to "do something" if I kept his kid on the sideline. He wore jersey number 32. That was a classic jersey number. The great Julius Erving, Malone, and Magic Johnson in the NBA would someday make that number iconic. Yet, CC stayed on the bench and we lost another game. The rest of the parents were beginning to look at me kind of strange. But I stood firm and held my ground. I made it crystal clear that everybody had to follow the same rules. No exceptions.

Afterwards, CC's father shadowed me into the parking lot. And in front of God and everybody who would listen…he let me have it. "What the hell are you tryin' to do Morris?"

"Nobody plays when they come late."

"Look, my son is carrying this sorry team!"

I turned my face towards him and calmly said, "Is that a fact?"

"Hell yeah it's a FACT…and if you don't start acting like you know what's best…"

I cut him off, "What's best is that you get out of my face… partner."

"Are you threatening me Coach?" I stepped real close to Big Clarence. He was in his mid-forties…and I couldn't be for certain that I could get the best of him…. but I was ready to find out. And he knew it. Instead of challenging me further he backed off.

He threw his son's uniform and it landed at my feet. "I'm done with this bullshit!!!"

"You're quitting, or CC's quitting?"

"What difference does it make, he's my son." Everyone stood waitin' to see what I was going to do or even say. I just leaned forward, picked it up and handed it to Maryam. And that was how she got on the team. She stood there and held onto it.

I faced the small crowd, "Anybody else got somethin' to say?"

We lost the first two games by a slim margin. After that, we stayed on top and almost took the championship. It was second place but the smiles on our faces said it was just as meaningful, if not even better.

"Is she still gloating over that trophy?"

"So Jazz, how are you feeling this morning?" I changed the subject.

"I'm fine. I felt a little queasy earlier..." It was official. My wife was pregnant again. Jasmine Morris was prettier than she'd ever been. She was showing right away this time. The subject of her going back to work was no longer an issue because she wanted to get a degree in Sociology and see where that leads her. "I found a nice day care, close to school for Halimah."

"That's great babe! I can pick you up first and we'll scoop Maryam up..."

She interrupted me, "Kareem, I want to get a car and drive...on my own." At that moment, I realized that I had been quarterbackin' every move. We had been ridin' together since the day we met. In actuality, I'd been way too protective. I asked her what she liked and I purchased a new platinum silver Mercedes station wagon. I couldn't wait to show her the Benz.

"It's your lucky day!"

"Okay," she responded without saying another word.

I jingled the keys teasingly, "You win...brand spanking new, it's a beauty."

Her eyes blinked hard, "You really bought the car?" She hugged me, then the kids piled on in a group hug. I stood out of her way as she opened the door releasing that leather seat aroma into our senses. You should have seen it. Jazz was like a kid in a candy store but this time, this kid owned it.

"I just asked for a station wagon, not a Mercedes."

Jasmine's eyes flooded with happy tears. "It's gorgeous… and the color, perfect!"

People didn't even try to hide it. As long as I was driving around town in my truck, with my wife and kids, and occasionally a couple boys on my basketball team, piled in like sardines, it was just fine. Nothing but love. But the minute I bought Jazz that Mercedes, to them, I'd crossed the line.

"You sure?"

"Yea, it's your car as much as it is mine," she laughed, "Besides, the team hasn't seen the car yet." I left the house that day feelin' a little uneasy, I just didn't know why.

ALTHEA JEWEL

TEN

I found a large parking spot. One that was far from the entrance and breathed in that new car smell. Grabbed my equipment bag, got out, secured the door and locked my new vehicle.

You know that feeling. I'm no different. I took a long look back, admiring my platinum beauty.

"Hello Coach," one of my team players jogged towards me dribbling his ball.

"Good morning Bobby, you're early, good to see you!"

He stopped bouncing the ball, held it to his side and came closer. "Wow, coach! Nice car!"

"Thank you, thank you, it's my wife's car." A few more people with their kids came and circled us, admiring the Benz.

Practice started as usual. There weren't any no shows. A productive morning. Almost immediately afterwards one of the parents approached me.

"Hey Curtis, I see you driving that Mercedes out there…" A tall man wearing a teal blue jogging suit and a baseball cap came closer. His belly was the biggest thing on his body. He chuckled, "I didn't picture you for a salesman…nice car," he nudged my arm, then came the expected, "They usually don't letcha' drive em' around on the weekends…how'd you pull that off?"

I continued walkin' but had slowed down just to comment to his nonsense. "Pull what off?" I said staring back at him, then added, "It's paid for." Now he's just lookin' like he wished he was a cop and he could make me show him my I.D.

"Oh," he says with a sheepish grin, adding, "Well, congratulations."

Sincere or not, at least it was a respectful comeback. By now, I've picked up my pace, Maryam still a few feet behind, finally caught up. All I could do was smile. Over time, off and on, more of the same. But it was different. It went from subtle, what I used to call "west coast jealousy" to out loud "who do you think you are" down south disharmony.

My dad once told me, "It doesn't matter how high you climb they'll always try to pull you down."

Pops refreshed my memory, "Curtis, it's a long way from over. I was born 1940, you in 63'. Yours in the 80's. And your grandkids haven't been born yet." That cut deep. Four-hundred-years and still counting on racism to be over with, keep counting.

Next Sunday Jasmine was shopping while I watched the children. Time passed and she wasn't home yet. I was a little bit concerned. Shortly afterwards, my wife came home in a AAA tow truck. She was shaken up and crying. Barefoot, I rushed outside to comfort her and carry our grocery bags inside.

"My car!" She was hysterical. "The windshield, bashed in completely…What's this world coming to?" She said some white guys and one Hispanic in their early 30's had been teasing her about her hijab on the way into the store, called her a colored nun.

From that day on, I escorted my wife and kids to the market. In fact, I worried if anyone confronted us would I over react or be calm? Was I going to have to drive around with a shotgun under my seat? Up until now, my experience living in the south was better than it was for me out west. My wife was askin' the wrong question. It wasn't, what's this world coming to, but more like, what are we going to do about it? And when?

"Maybe we should just move back to California?" Jazz asked, sounding desperate.

"And live in a three-bedroom apartment with the neighbors too close for comfort, lucky to have a balcony because we can't afford a backyard?" The conversation came up several times that night.

"My stepdad would help us get a nice house."

I was packing tobacco in my pipe looking out our bedroom window. "Oh my God, Jazz, really, it's come to this again?"

She kept on fluffing out the bedsheets and continued, "Yea Kareem, maybe you need to listen to YOURSELF sometimes," she smirked, "And learn how to swallow your pride."

"Uh oh, here we go," I picked up my lighter and kept packing my tobacco.

She blinked her eyes, exaggerating her next comment, "Ever since you bought that damn car!"

I didn't even respond. If that's the way she really feels, then there's no discussion needed. We tippy-toed around each other for the next few days. I didn't want to talk. Neither did she. I took solitude in my back yard. I reclined in my hammock and looked out at the same landscape that once gave me peace and tranquility. Now it was just a lot of trees in a big empty space.

Who is this woman I married? Where is the Jasmine I fell in love with? I know relationships have ups and downs. What happened? And I'm sick of people saying "it's just postpartum"...when male testosterone is kickin' in and I have my needs, I'm insensitive.

But I didn't want to get ahead of myself. I go back to construction whenever I need a new perspective on things. New focus. New satisfaction. Let's work on this house. I could improve on something that might make me feel better about my relationship. Yea, that's what I do. Fellas, whenever you find yourself in a situation that's similar to mine. Get your tools ready. I'm observing my life the way an astronomer peers through a telescope. I'm on the boat and I'm looking for any sign of hope to keep this damn thing afloat.

I tapped the bottom of my pipe onto the ashtray, cleaned it out and added more of that sweet cherry tobacco. I talk a lot of yakety yak but I love my wife. I wanted to make it work. I wanted those history books to tell a different story about Black families. In particular Black men.

When I was younger, livin' in Cerritos, pops told me about the government plan to keep Black families apart. Told our young women, "What do you need a man for?" And welfare took our place at the head of the table. Our women put us out in the street because we couldn't keep a job.

Pops would say, "Yeah, Miss Independent, put that Negro out." I could see that playing out. But for now, my theme song was still on Al Green "Let's Stay Together" and I was gonna play it over and over and over again…until I couldn't play it no more.

I heard a flock of birds pass over the treetops in the distance. That night I decided to call a contractor and get a bid on adding something new…something for all of us, not just for me. I was going to have the best Olympic-sized pool, actually the only one, so far on the whole block. A week later, the contractor met me at our house to draw up the plans. He was the father of a guy I'd met on one of my construction sites. An Armenian cat from New York. He was cool. I told him about some of the trouble we'd had with the neighbors. The time our windshield got bashed out at the supermarket. He said to call him, day or night, if anything else popped off he'd have my back. Nice gesture. But I knew that if anything happened, by the time he got here, it would be too late.

I kept a firearm out back, in a place where no one else could put their hands on it. I heard too many stories about guns. People leaving them around the house, a child gets a hold of it, a tragedy waiting to happen. Or maybe an enraged spouse, loses their mind and pulls the trigger…over some bullshit. Naw, I wasn't havin' it. Even still, I realized that what was going on deep down, was bigger than me. I couldn't shake it. For the past few years, I'd prayed five times a day, building up my discipline. I still wasn't prepared on what needs to happen next. That Friday, I went to the masjid, for Jumah prayer.

"Brother Kareem, good to see you." No pictures on the walls. Just a soothing shade of greyish green with white crown molding. Also, one beautiful textured wall with an Arabic plaque to the right of the Imam's podium. The room was about 2,000 square feet with spaced out rows of Mediterranean prayer rugs on top of the plush grey carpet, facing east. I smiled, placing my shoes on the top rack, where I always do, then found my way to an open prayer spot. I prayed silently while prostrating, giving honor to God, as I bent down and touched my forehead to the rug beneath me.

There were less than fifty people, with women and children on one side, and men on the other. Jazz used to question the reason why we worshipped that way. I figured it was just a tradition and that's not why I come to Jumah. Her rationale was just a Western-civilization distraction tactic. The Prophets spoke of this in their teachings. I saw familiar faces and some I hadn't seen before. Everyone was on the same accord. We were a family.

The Imam spoke for about forty minutes. That was considered an average time to speak. Afterwards the men conversated, caught up on things, while families greeted in the foyer and headed out into the parking lot filled with children's laughter. Others went next door to the Muslim restaurant and had an early dinner along with a slice of the best pastry in town. Everything was in unison.

Everyone wanted to know how my wife and kids were doing. They were especially inquisitive about Maryam. I was so preoccupied with my own soul searching that it wasn't obvious. But not long after that, my eyes were opened. Maryam was meticulous about everything related to sports. She practiced every day. I had to build a half-court out back and installed illuminated outdoor lights so she could practice. That girl had skills. And she could dunk on any boy in the city. It's too bad the WNBA didn't start until 1996, when she graduated from high school. Long before that, she rode her bike around the neighborhood. Jazz gave her a little leeway to go around the block and back.

And that's when Maryam started hangin' with her closest friend, a Hispanic girl, named Regina. But everybody, besides me, called her Reggie. Almost every day, she rang our doorbell looking for Maryam to walk her black poodle with our dogs. They were good friends…that's what we assumed.

Jazz and I were happily married. Two years passed and then the honeymoon crumbled. Arguing by day. Sexual tension by night. It became routine. Just act like everything is still cool. But it's not.

And then came what should've been the obvious. She was pregnant again. "Congratulations Mrs. Morris, you're having twins!"

I can't lie, it felt like a gut punch. Nervously I reacted in complete silence. Jasmine's dimpled smile prevailed, "Curtis? You going to be alright?"

Jazz was a vibrant thirty-four-year-old woman with an old lady mentality. Every day, she looked in the mirror and gave me that woe is me facial expression. Like this was the end and she would never recover. I saw her go from a little upset to depression. I tried to encourage her, "Come on baby, let's go for a peaceful walk."

But she rarely went anywhere with this pregnancy. After the first couple of months, Jazz seemed to be consistently moody and tired all the time. I hired a housekeeper to help out at the house. Her name was Mrs. Johnson. A sweet old southern gal who loved takin' care of kids. She prepared all the meals, did most of the laundry, and babysat the children while I was away at work during the day.

It was February 3, 1988. Jasmine was seven-and-a-half months pregnant and she woke me up from a weary sleep, "Kareem," she nudged me, "Wake up…my water broke."

"Isn't it too soon?" I sprung up, wide-eyed and reached for my coat and car keys.

"I know… she sounded afraid, "But it's time."

The housekeeper stayed at the house while I eased my wife into the back seat of the sedan. I put my hazard lights on and sped off to the hospital, twenty minutes away.

An hour later, just before dawn, Jazz went into full labor. With Halimah the birth was smooth. Not this time around. Jazz screamed out in a lot of pain. They rushed her in for an emergency delivery and I was told to be calm and wait outside. The doors to the operating room swung back and I just stood there, gasping for breath. I watched to see if I could get a glimpse of what was going on. I saw them moving away from me. People that had been next to me, now were out of my view. Just like when my sister was in the hospital…that same anxious feeling of not knowing what was next came over me.

The nurse finally called me, gave me a gown to put on, and walked me to the recovery room. Jazz was hooked up to an IV and some type of monitor, constantly beeping while she slept.

I immediately asked, "Why is she hooked up to a monitor like that?"

I mean she looked really bad. It took me back. I didn't realize I was crying but tears rushed down the side of my face. It was a normal reaction.

The surgeon called me to step outside of the recovery room. "Your wife and daughter will be fine."

"What does that mean?"

"We did everything we could…I'm so sorry Mr. Morris, we…we…we, couldn't save the boy." I must've passed out. I don't remember anything except the words the doctor told me.

"Mr. Morris, we gave you a mild sedative to…" It felt dark and cold even with the brightness of the sun shining in from the window.

"Where's my wife?" I sat up, checked my watch, it was almost noon.

The nurse answered, "Resting in her room."

I wiped my face with a towel and followed the nurse back down the hallway. Jasmine was laying on the bed, holding our newborn daughter. She looked over at me, her eyes puffy trying to keep it together. I knelt down next to her bed and caressed her face. I told her how beautiful she was. How proud I was for her birthing our child.

"I'm sorry Kareem."

"Shhh, rest now, save your strength." She closed her eyes and drifted back off, sleeping, while I held our newborn daughter. Later that day, I called home and my Aunt Lorraine answered. She sent Mrs. Johnson, the housekeeper home. Then reassured me that the kids were doing fine.

Two days later, me, Jasmine, and baby Naomi returned home. We'd already bought two bassinets. I lifted the one that our son would never lie in and set it back down. That was a breaking point for me. I turned out all the lights and tippy toed into the shower so I wouldn't wake anyone.

My newborn daughter and my wife slept soundly in our bed. And once I got into the water, while the warmth of the steam comforted me, I cried, silently, until my chest hurt. Jazz became my rock again. She insisted that she would be fine. But how could that be?

Whenever Naomi cried, Jazz would say something like, "Mama knows you miss your brother." And then she would kiss the baby and say, "He's in heaven…don't you cry."

She was in her own world. Her mother even stayed with us for a couple weeks. Aunt Lorraine came by every day except weekends. Mrs. Johnson took care of our household. Cooking. Cleaning. Washing diapers.

Another month passed before Jasmine started interacting with all of us again. I was grateful it hadn't been any longer. Just at the beginning of spring, fate granted me a custody hearing for Aaron. I'd taken an early flight to Los Angeles. I took a yellow cab straight to the downtown courthouse. As usual the traffic was rough and my cab driver didn't seem to know where he was going.

"Just turn on, here, on First Street," I told him. I was alone that day. Just hours ago, I told Jazz to not worry about comin' with me. I would not have my family trekked across the country. Especially, not now. Besides, it was just a turnaround flight. Get in that morning. And fly back home that same night. The weather in Los Angeles did not disappoint me. The sun found its way across my shaven face. It felt good. Today it was all on the line. And I was prepared for the outcome.

We were the first to be heard. As I walked in, the entire Whitfield family had arrived before me. To my surprise, Traci was there next to Allison. I called them the wrecking crew. Bernard and Kaye Whitfield and my son Aaron. Aaron was clutching onto Allison's mother, Kaye, his grandmother, like he was about to be snatched up by immigration. It was supposed to be a set up.

ALTHEA JEWEL

ELEVEN

All eyes on me. I spoke but none replied. I greeted them anyway, "Good morning." My voice carried and Aaron let go of his grandmother's hand, and smiled at me. They hadn't turned him against me yet. Everything was going to be alright.

After the mediator, Mrs. Parker, introduced herself and explained why we're here, the room was silent for a brief moment. "Judge, I don't feel that this man should be granted ANY custody," Mrs. Whitfield spoke out of turn.

"This man?" Mrs. Parker asked, adjusting her glasses as she examined Allison's mother. By then, Traci and Mrs. Whitfield whispered something and Traci grabbed Aaron's hand, escorting him towards the exit door. The sound of her heels tapped the floor as they trailed off.

Mrs. Whitfield finally answered, "I am the child's maternal grandmother..."

There we were. All dressed up in our Sunday best. Testifying. Hoping that a court of law could do for us what we were not grown up enough to do on our own. I scratched the top of my head and looked straight at her when she took her jab at me.

Kaye Whitfield, continued, "Curtis is only a father by DNA…he is not good for my grandson."

The mediator spoke in my defense. "Good, you at least agree with the paternity findings…now ma'am please be seated." The mediator continued, "Well, Mr. Morris, have you been paying child support?"

"Yes," I answered and nodded my head.

"Yes, I see, you've been paying for over four years."

"Six years Mrs. Parker."

She looked through the paperwork and corrected herself, "Yes, it has been six years."

The Whitfield's gaze carried no weight to my receipts. I cleared my throat and stood with my shoulder's back, waitin' on the outcome.

"And you live in Atlanta Georgia Mr. Morris?"

"Yes, I am married and have a stable home there."

Mr. Whitfield shouted out like a heckler in a barn fight, "Married? You never married my daughter!" I didn't even turn around to look at him.

"Mrs. Parker, I proposed to my ex but we broke up before making it official."

The mediator looked at me and then back at the Whitfield bunch. "I've seen a lot of families in the past fifteen years," she said holding her chin, "I just don't understand why so many unnecessary obstacles…we cannot agree on how to raise these innocent children." She went on to say, "Who is Aaron's mother, Allison Whitfield?"

Allison up to now had remained silent. "Yes, I'm his mother…Allison Whitfield."

"What do you have to say about all this?"

Allison looked straight ahead at the mediator and said, "He's not a bad person."

"So why did you bring your entire family here, when the matter is between you, your child, and the child's father?"

"They are my witnesses." Allison shot back in her normal exaggerated tone.

"I don't like public theater Miss Whitfield," she raised her voice to Allison's level, "What have they witnessed?"

At twenty-five, I could honestly say that the three years age difference between us was never a factor. I stood there thinkin' about how since the beginning, Allison had made it up in her head that somehow, those thirty-six months between our ages was a big deal. I'd lived just as hard and learned even more lessons than her. Allison glanced at me then turned and looked to her parents for answers.

"Okay, I see where this is going...everyone, leave the room except Miss Whitfield and Mr. Morris." And that's how it started. Joint custody. As long as I wasn't endangering Aaron and kept up my child support, then I could finally have my son back in my life. It was my absolute parental right. Pay close attention now. I said absolute right.

"Curtis that's wonderful news!" That's all Ma said when anything was going my way. I was just hoping it would stay true.

Allison and I were on speaking terms again. Per the court's order, since so much time had passed and I lived in another state, we'd first get local visits once or twice a month at my parent's house. We agreed to once a month for starters, since I lived some distance. As soon as it felt right, he could fly with me to Atlanta and start our summer and every other holiday visitation. But for now, I traveled to California, to his comfort zone. I would spend Friday night to Sunday morning with him at my folks. Ma would whip up her special breakfast and I'd prepare the fruit bowl. Sliced melon, pineapple and strawberries. Aaron loved strawberries. He was getting to know us all over again. He was comfortable with the arrangement and so was I.

For years, Ma hadn't been able to clear out Waleena's room. She held onto all her things. Seemed like the memory of my sister's passing was being preserved in a time capsule. One day, after Aaron went back to Allison's house, Ma asked me what I'd been waiting to hear for a long time.

"Curtis, can you go to the store and bring me some moving boxes?"

"I'll be right back Ma, anything else you need?"

"No, that will be just fine."

"Okay Ma." By the time I came back to the house, Ma had already started clearing the closet. She'd set neat piles of items on the bedroom floor. We worked together deciding what would go and what keepsakes would remain. I could feel the tension ease up in the room little by little.

"I guess I was holding on too long," Ma said tearfully.

I hugged her, real tight and said, "Keep her close to your heart Ma, that's where she belongs." I called Jasmine and told her I wouldn't be home until Tuesday, after I finished helping my folks with my sister's room.

"Why do you have to babysit your mother?"

"You know what Jazz...I'll see you when I get there." I stayed two extra days just to show Jasmine that her lack of sensitivity wasn't helping. Ma gave everything away, except for a few things and my sister's track trophies. After the Salvation Army truck drove away from the house, me and pops prepped the room to start painting.

"I got it after this son, you go on back home in the morning...I still remember how to paint." We laughed. I was a little embarrassed that my folks heard the tone in my voice when I last spoke with Jasmine on the phone.

The next morning, I took a flight back to Atlanta. There was no further discussion after I got home. Time passed quickly. It was already winter. I was still back and forth between Atlanta and Los Angeles. It was like finding an invisible needle in a haystack to get Jasmine to cut me some slack. "You have to trust me on this Jazz."

"I do trust you."

"Jazz if you trusted me, you wouldn't call me every thirty minutes when I leave. I'm just tryin' to get Aaron back. Remember? You suggested I do this." She was just getting out the shower, towel dried quickly and put on her night gown. I pulled her close to me, "Hey...I'm doing this so we can all be family."

She withdrew from my touch. I wasn't going to fight her on it anymore. In the past, I would wait for her to cool off and then I'd make an effort. But she wanted to be left alone. So be it.

Our youngest, Nee Nee, as we called her, was already crawling. Even to the front door if we weren't being watchful. Halimah, now two, the quiet one, followed ten-year-old

Maryam everywhere. Maryam was my helpmate. Everywhere I needed her to be at home, she was. And I know she was sensitive to the fact that her mother and I were not gettin' along. She was the peacemaker. Or at least she tried to be.

One day after my weekend in California, exhausted, I stayed in bed the whole day. When I woke up, I reached for the phone and noticed a book on the nightstand, next to my wife's side of the bed.

First of all, I know I was wrong, violatin' privacy is ugly. God knows if she ever looked through my phone, or my truck for some random type crap I would be pissed. But honestly, going through her notebook, was not my intention. But you know what they say, if you're lookin' for something, don't be surprised when you find it. I opened up a page towards the end and this is what she wrote.

For a long time, I wondered why I was an only child. I promised myself that when I grew up, I wouldn't place that worrisome burden on my children. I wanted a big family. But now I see why mom kept it simple. It's not that I'm not grateful for my kids. I love them. I just don't have any energy anymore and I feel myself slipping further away from my husband. The last time we made love I just laid there, closed my eyes, and imagined myself far away, on the beach, listening to the ocean. By the time the sunsets, thankfully, it's over.

Thankfully it's over? That's what Jazz is thinking when I'm touching, holding, caressing and makin' love to her? Or let me set the record straight - I've been makin' love to her. Worn out. Calloused hands. Sore feet. Back almost ready to go out...and still, makin' love to my wife is totally energizing.

And now I find out it's much deeper. I shouldn't have kept reading but now I'm lookin' for answers...so I turned the page...and continued...

ALTHEA JEWEL

TWELVE

I'm devastated, she writes, and Curtis doesn't seem to care about me losing the baby. Not even a simple ceremony for some closure. I regret not making him agree to something. I thank Allah for saving Naomi. But I carry Nolan in my thoughts every day. That was his name.

My husband is consumed with this fight for his first son Aaron. But it seems like a war that he isn't winning. It feels like he's replaced Nolan with his own son. And I am beginning to resent him for that. Leaving me alone in this house to deal with everything isn't right. Sometimes I feel like I'm a single parent again. Why did I even get married?

Then I read the last entry again and again and again. Why did I even get married? That was it. I set the notebook down on the nightstand. My hands got sweaty and my jawbone tightened. At first, I wanted to confront her, in fact, I needed to confront her, but not right now. Right now, would be me shakin' her like a tree until half the leaves fell off. And that might end me up in jail. I've never been to jail before. I wasn't ready to find out what that felt like…not today.

I bowed my head and I prayed. Not a Muslim prayer, but a fast old fashioned Christian style one. On my knees. On my side of the bed. God, please forgive me for reading my wife's diary. God please don't let me confront this woman today. God please hear my prayer and work everything out for Your good. Then I got off my knees. Took a few sips of my bottled water and went back to sleep. I slept peacefully.

Must've been an hour or so later when I woke to the sound of Jazz calling out my Christian name. "Curtis!" I didn't answer her. It felt strange at first. But I had to start doing things differently. She got louder, "If you've had enough sleep can you come down here… please?"

I stretched and stood up walking towards the hallway. I took one last look at the pink and purple flower design on the cover of that trifling woman's book, then walked slowly downstairs. All the action was going on in my kitchen. Of course, the baby's crying. Babies are supposed to cry. But thinkin' back over the past year, Naomi was picking up on Jasmine's energy. That same ugly energy Jazz has been expressing in her notebook.

"Can you hold the baby?"

"Jazz, it's Monday…I overslept," I picked up baby Naomi and she stopped crying. Rubbed the side of her puffy face, wiped her tears, then I said, "I have to go to work."

Jazz was puttin' away groceries and placed a bag of dog food next to the sliding glass door. "Jazz call Mrs. Johnson and ave her work full-time around here for a while."

She finally looked at me, "I don't want some other woman unning my household."

"Come on now. You and Mrs. Johnson get along just fine... all her!" Now she's walking towards me confrontational while 'm holding the baby.

"Kareem, you just got back from Los Angeles and you aven't spent any time here with us."

"Jasmine, I thought you supported me on getting Aaron, when did that change?" She was stackin' the food in the pantry with her back towards me.

"Oh, now I'm the one not being supportive," she laughed. She turned her body at an angel towards me and said loudly, "You see Kareem, that's your problem! Always spreading yourself too thin!"

Maryam came inside from the back yard with two empty dog bowls. "Mama what's wrong?"

Jasmine's vibe changed, "Who said anything's wrong?"

Maryam didn't hesitate, "Then why are you yellin'?"

"Maryam, go to your room, I need to talk with Kareem alone. Please."

I immediately interrupted her, "Not now Jazz... but WE DO need to talk."

Jasmine's eyes flashed when she heard those words, "We need to talk, really?"

Maryam took the baby from my arms and walked towards her room. I looked away from Jasmine, repeating myself, "Yea, really."

In hindsight, that was the day my heart broke. It moved me

from I do, to I won't…would we ever be the same again? You know, as men, we know, going into a relationship it's different when you're sittin' down compared to when you're standin' up. We don't realize when the road ahead looks uneven. We're comfortable stayin' off the road, sittin' at home until the leg of the chair is feeling wobbly.

The rest of us, well we think too logically to worry about what's outside of the box. No speculating. No what ifs. Worry about that bridge when we cross it. You know who we are. The good men. The predictable ones. He's going to marry. He's going to provide. And ladies, please don't hate me for sayin' this. But no matter how attractive you think you are…once you muck it up, you don't need a crystal ball to see that he's going to take back his last name. You're not leavin' him any other choice.

I went on to work that Monday, determined to not let my wife's foolishness get in the way of my business. In fact, she made me hypersensitive to work even harder. All the energy I'd focused on her, I transferred it to being better at my job. My mood went from, thinkin' about getting home to her; to, can't wait to lock the door behind me and get gone. Tension never subsides, it always builds.

Fellas, that's your first sign that she's playin' a game. Now you're just roommates but you're payin' all the bills. You never needed her for finances. But the groceries, the household supplies, she's stopped contributing and slacked off lookin' after the kids. I became Mr. Mom, with a wife?

I pulled a load of clothes out of the dryer that had been

in there since the day before yesterday…all my work clothes, wrinkled, pants half a shade lighter, and half a size smaller when I tried to put them on.

The sound of the washing machine in the background with water filling up for the rinse cycle. Jazz and I remained civil for the next few months. But it was obvious, we were not even close to being close anymore. I stopped doin' things for her and as I already said, she stopped doin' a lot of things for me. Finally, I got the go ahead to bring Aaron home to start visitation.

ALTHEA JEWEL

THIRTEEN

The night before my departure and I just couldn't sleep. You know when you're restless, everything in the middle of the night seems louder. The house settling. From the den the refrigerator sounds intensify. The clock on the far wall, tickin' was insane.

I turned the television on, kept the volume low. Although my folks had never split up, I remember my pops watching television alone in the den…with the volume turned down. I knew him and Ma had a "disagreement" as they called it. And I remember tryin' to make light of it and told him he should turn on some good music and fire up a joint.

He'd say, "Boy you better never bring no weed up inside this house, I'll knock you out." I was just kidding but now as a man, sleepin' on my own couch, I see why he didn't find that joke funny.

There I was, alone in the dark, anxious about tomorrow. I don't know what I was watchin'. I just lay there staring at the set. I fell asleep and then Maryam came in the room around 6:30 that next morning and shut the television off. She gave me a smile and walked back down the hallway towards the stairs. I could hear the baby crying and Jazz giving her some instructions before I got up and got dressed to go to the airport.

It was overcast that morning. It reminded me of those mornings when I was a kid on the way to track practice with my sister. We had our whole lives ahead of us. That was so long ago.

At the airport, I checked in one bag, only because I had a gift for my father. I bought him a pinstripe suit with a vest. It was really sharp. Dark grey, his favorite color.

The flight was peaceful. It wasn't crowded. Everyone was courteous. Still, it didn't put me in a better mood. I should have been on top of the world that day. But I kept playin' the last few weeks with Jasmine over and over again in my head. And my back ached from sleeping on the couch.

At baggage claim, I watched the luggage go around for what seemed like forever. People who'd come after me were gettin' their bags and I was still standin' there. Waiting. I looked down at my watch and it was almost 10:30, I was supposed to be at my folks at 11:00. To meet Aaron shortly afterwards. I was beginning to feel anxious. Maybe I should just leave the bag and find it on the way back home. A few minutes later, I spotted my luggage bag and headed outside the terminal to grab a cab. Wow. Where the cabs usually line up, not one in sight.

First thing I hear is a horn blowin' and a male voice callin', "Curtis! Hey, Curtis!" It was Marvin Whitfield drivin' a shiny new black Chevy truck with a cab on the back.

"Hey Marvin, what are you doing here?" He pulled up to he loadin' zone where I was standing and motioned for me to get in. I always run into somebody I know in L.A. so it wasn't o awkward runnin' into him.

"You sure?" I asked as I accepted his offer to drive me to ny folks' house.

"Unless you waitin' on Jesus," he laughed, "Get in...it's the east I can do for you, partner."

"This you?" I asked, approvingly about the truck, ignoring his previous comment.

"Yeah, I bought it for Cookie, but she never drives it, I love t." I nodded complimenting him again.

Marvin quickly, actually too quickly, offered to take my uggage bag and place it in back for me. He smiled and said, "I love this truck, there's room in places I didn't even know about."

I turned my attention to the time and told him, "I gotta pick up Aaron after I see my folks."

He shifted into drive, engine revved and we took off. "Yea, I heard. You gettin' to see your boy, that's good news."

"Thanks," I said as the truck idled at a red light.

"Don't worry partner, we'll make it there in less than thirty minutes!"

"Naw man, don't drive fast, I was just lettin' you know," I grinned. I thought to myself, I guess the family told him I was coming...I let it go. I glanced over my shoulder and couldn't see where he'd put my bag. Seemed kinda odd why he didn't just put it on the back seat where I could just grab it.

Heading south on the 405, Marvin with his usual too much talk, "Wow Curtis! Small world!" He was laughing and nervously tappin' his hand on the steering wheel. That's when I got a really good look at him. His clothes were not fresh. His eyes. Either jet lagged or high on something. Maybe a little bit of both.

"So, Marvin, you still workin'?"

He stuttered, "Aww oh, still have my company but I haven't worked in a minute."

He sounded nervous, "You know, construction… sometimes slow."

"Yea," I said, "Why didn't you call? I know some guys down here that hire for short-term gigs." No comment. He signaled to change lanes.

"How's your wife doing Curtis?"

"She's good."

"The kids?"

"Good." He kept looking in his rear mirror. Like he was lookin' for something…someone. We get on the next freeway and I spot a Union 76 gas station off an exit.

He spotted it too. "Aww man, you mind if we stop real quick and get some gas?"

"Yea, okay."

I couldn't shake the weird vibe I was feelin'. As soon as we pulled into the station's lot a dark colored car pulled up with police sirens going off. Three quick times with their lights flashing. "Are they flashin' at us?"

"Damn Curtis. I been thinkin' bout how to change this thang up…it wasn't supposed to go down like this."

I just froze in my seat gazing at that big orange 76 ball… round and round. I sat motionless in the truck while another police car pulled up, officers exiting wearin' black DEA vests.

"Really Marvin? Drug enforcement?" Marvin seemed shaken but unapologetic. I just couldn't believe what was happening.

The cop on the left walked towards the driver side and the one on the right...well he was focusing on me. "Get out!"

The other chimed in, hand on his holster and told me, "Put your hands where I can see them and exit the vehicle." I got out the truck and he immediately cuffed me and motioned for me to sit down on the curb. I'd never been in trouble with the law before. And I just kept thinkin' about the sound when they cuff you. It's a grinding metal, scraping, it makes you feel like a bear in a trap. It echoed in my head for a minute. And then I forgot about it, too worried about when they'd be taking these shits off.

They were askin' Marvin a lot of questions and he wasn't givin' any answers. They slung his ass down on the concrete... then started searching the truck.

"Don't you need a search warrant?" I asked, foolishly.

"They've been following," Marvin said quietly.

"Negro! You knew you were being followed and you let me get in the truck with you?"

"Shh keep it down," he said, "I thought I could outrun them."

"By stopping?"

One of the police came back towards us to see what we were arguing about. He was chewing gum and said to me, "Looks like your friend here got you in a bit of a pickle."

I remained quiet. But my blood was boiling. I'm not getting my son today. Maybe never. My luggage bag had been opened up and they'd rummaged through my things…and pulled somethin' out from it. I strained to see what they were laughing so loud about.

"Well, well, well, what do we have here?" The senior agent waved a plastic baggy at us. Marvin's face looked funny. And he wouldn't look at me. That's when I knew he did it.

"So cuz, you gonna let me go to jail for your bullshit?" I told him.

"Naw Curtis…you don't understand, I had no choice." They put us side by side in the back of that police car, on purpose so we could fight. I head butted him so hard that I heard his nose pop, blood streaming all over the both of us. The police found that entertaining.

"Damn! You boys gotta behave back there, save it for the holding tank." We went backwards. Back north. Destination downtown county jail. They booked us. Felony possession of illegal drugs…heroine. A drug I'd never even seen before. They said it was practically pure, uncut, whatever that means. Marvin Whitfield had managed in less than an hour, to do what I would have rather taken my chances on doing myself, ruining my life. If you've ever been to jail you won't forget the way you felt or how you were treated. You remember every bead of sweat that fell from your body. You'll remember your heart poundin' and feeling like a fugitive when they take your mug shot.

You know, life is about preparation. You can handle situations better if you're prepared for what is about to happen. Nothing worse than to wake up and find yourself in the middle of somebody else's bullshit. Yea, I know that it was 1988. I remember that it was the month of May. Going to jail made me a statistic. Thankfully, I lived to tell my story. Everybody isn't that fortunate. RIP to all the ones who died at the hands of animalistic brutality. So, in retrospect, I was one of the lucky ones.

I let my wrists go limp when they took my fingerprints. I breathed in and out slowly when they asked to take my wallet and personal belongings. I felt violated when I was strip searched but just to get it over with, I didn't react.

Two detectives, I didn't bother to get their names, took me to a small room and questioned me. "Well, looks like you got yourself into some messy business."

"This isn't my business," I said in a sobering tone.

"Well, Curtis, you and your friend didn't get to quite finish that business, did you?"

The other detective cut in, "Look, if it isn't yours…just tell us where or who you got it from and we'll go easy on you."

I held my head down, "I don't know anybody. I was on my way to pick up my son and go back home to Atlanta." I was led back to an empty room with a metal bench and told to wait. I didn't question them I just sat on the bench and waited.

Early the next morning, I got a tray of mush, I couldn't eat, but I did get to call my folks. Exhausted and embarrassed, I waited for my dad to answer, "Hello."

"Pop, sorry to just now be calling you."

"Where are you? What happened son?" I told him where I was and as much as I knew about how I got arrested.

"Marvin?" my father said nervously, "Whose Marvin?"

"You know… Marvin. Allison's cousin Marvin."

"Aww Curtis, no, not more of this Whitfield shit!"

Frustrated I twisted the telephone cord and tried to drown out the noise around me. "Look pops. I have a short time on this phone. But I need you to do something for me. Call my friend Ahmad and ask him to hire me an attorney. I'll pay him back but I have to get out of this place."

My father's voice sounded strained, "Everybody's been calling for you. Jasmine, Allison, and some lady from the courthouse called...okay...I'll call Ahmad and ask him for you."

"Thank you pops. And call Alee, just tell her I'm sorry, and I'll let you know what happens as soon as I find something out."

"Son, if you don't get this mess straightened out...you'll lose Aaron."

"I know pops, I know."

There came the awkward pause before I added, "Please ask Aunt Lorraine if she can go over my house, to tell my wife, I'm in jail, in person." Tell her in person. That's what people do when something tragic happens and they don't want to give you the news in a letter or over the telephone. I wasn't dead...it just felt like it.

My father paused, "Okay, I'll have your mother take care of that."

"Tell Ma to get her prayer warriors on top of this...this mess."

"Oh, she's already on top of it."

"Thank you," I said, "Don't worry, everything's gonna be alright." But it wasn't alright. The police said I had to prove it.

he custody court said I had to prove it. To be honest, how do
ou prove you're innocent when everybody already thinks the
worst of you. Even I knew that the truth was just a Hail Mary...
and I'm not Catholic.

A week later my attorney, Mr. Willoughby, came to
he county jail to talk to me. "Mr. Morris," he said, "Based
on everything so far, the worst that can happen to you is
probation."

I sat on the edge of a metal seat, smiling at this thirty-
something-year-old Black man in a dark blue business suit. His
confidence level was impressive from the get go. But my first
reaction, honestly, how old is this cat? Am I his first client?

I thought a minute, then said, "What do you mean, the
worst?" Willoughby told me that most people underestimate
him because of his age. At forty, he'd been in business as a
defense attorney for over ten years.

"I know it's hard for you to trust anybody but Curtis, just
hear me out." He schooled me that day. He said jail is just a
revolving door. People go in, people get out, and the most of
the same people go back in again. "The driver, Marvin, will do
some time. He was under narcotics radar and he has priors."

"Yea, but I was with him."

"Curtis, you seem like a reasonable guy. No criminal
record. No prior convictions elsewhere? No trouble with the
law. And if your wife still wants to divorce you after this...she
probably wasn't going to stay with you anyway." Damn that
cut deep.

A correctional officer walked casually past me, glanced us

over and kept walking. "I believe in you Morris," he went on to say, "The problem is the amount of what they found warrants scrutiny." Willoughby smiled, waited for my response.

I squinted my eyes and asked him, "What do you mean?"

"If they'd found a smaller amount, a gram or so, then it's possession. But four-and-a-half ounces, that's possession with intent to sell."

He had my full attention. "Sell? They charged me with sales? I have never ever touched drugs!"

I pounded my fist on the counter, "Naw….naw…let's take it to trial, I'm innocent!"

"This case, carries seven to twenty years and if you want to fight it, since they consider you a flight risk, there's no bail. You'll sit in here another year maybe, just waiting on your trial to start."

"So…Mr. Willoughby, what are you saying?"

"I don't recommend trial. A jury of your peers…risky. If you were older, with priors, we'd have to fight or you'd never get out. I get paid more if you fight. But the odds of winning this case are not favorable."

My voice cracked, "But I'm innocent."

"I wish I could tell you that innocence wins cases, but it doesn't," he said solemnly. He explained the strategy and even though it wasn't what I wanted to hear, it made sense.

"You want me to plead no contest and get out without fighting it."

"I want you to do what you're comfortable with. I'm just giving you advice on the best way moving forward."

"Damn, but I didn't do anything wrong…it's his shit, I

never touched the stuff."

"Marvin is sticking to his lie that you were aware of the drugs...they found them in your luggage bag."

"Wait?" I blurted out, "He moved my bag and now he's putting this on me?"

"Keep your voice down Mr. Morris. And yes, he is denying everything. Saying you brought the drugs from Atlanta before he picked you up from the airport."

"What?"

"If you're clean and there's nothing happening back at home, you have nothing to worry about. DEA will probably follow you around after this, for a short while, and when they see nothing is going on they'll keep you in the database, like everybody else who comes through here...but once they see it's a dead end, they'll drop it."

"If I ever get out of here, the only dead end will be Marvin!"

"Don't kid around like that Morris, if you want this to be over. After it's all behind you, your best bet is to stay clear of him and anyone affiliated with that family." There was a row of us. In orange jumpsuits. On visits with loved ones and people seeing legal aide to try to get the best advice and the most comfort. It was a vulnerable position, sitting between the glass and your comforter. I sat takin' it all in, thinking what to say next.

Then I asked him what I'd been wantin' to know all along, "But my son? Six years to finally get him back in my life!"

"How old is your son?"

"He's six..."

"You have custody?"

"I was supposed to be picking him up the day I got caught up in this mess."

"Oh," he said with a frown on his face, "How's your relationship been with your ex?"

"You want the truth?"

"Nothing but headaches."

It felt good to get it all off my chest. I even thanked him for listening, even told him about Traci. He paused a real long minute, "I want to tell you a little something about me."

"Yea."

"About five years before I finished law school, I was dating this girl and we fell in love…for sure, I was in love. And when she took me home to meet her parents in Boston, I realized how small the world is and even how smaller people's minds are. You know the story…I'm Black, she's White, nobody wants to experience that Guess Who's Coming To Dinner…not in real life."

After Willoughby told his story I realized that folks from Boston were just like Alee's folks…but mine felt worse. "So, I don't belong in her world?"

"I'm not saying that Curtis," he sighed, "But I am saying that it's probably not a coincidence that the family who wanted you out, is involved in your downfall."

"Just think about it," he went on to say, "You got custody, making you tied to them for the next decade, even longer, and they wanted nothing to do with you. And now you're locked up because you took a ride with your ex's cousin."

I felt pressure rising in my chest, "I took Marvin into my

home and helped him get a job."

"You should feel responsible for your kid...but this is just somebody getting back at you because they can't control you." I tried to swallow but my mouth felt drier than cotton.

"Curtis, I did a little digging before I came to see you. There was an anonymous phone call to the airport police the day before you and Marvin got picked up. Warning them that some drug activity was going down. They didn't give any names but said to follow a suspect from Atlanta."

"What?"

"General description of what you looked like and what type of truck you'd be riding in. It appears to be a coordinated effort. Planned. I don't know if Marvin was in on it...probably just used him to get to you."

Immediately I thought about how the Whitfield's acted in court the day I got custody. Is this revenge? "I never even thought about it like that."

"All I know, is people have different motivations for doing things. I just need you to stay away from Marvin if you run into him in here. And don't talk to anyone about your case. If the ex comes down here to visit you, refuse to see her. Let me deal with the custody issue. I can get things postponed until you're ready to make a decision on leaving those people alone...or not."

I was speechless. The phone call cut off by the visitation buzzer. Totally stunned. I stared and watched him place the phone on the receiver and told me to stay strong.

You hear guys bragging about how they'd never been to jail. Like it was a badge of honor. Somehow, they'd managed not to entangle themselves with the law. All along breakin' laws, just haven't crapped out at the table…didn't stay too long at the thug party, wouldn't be in a position such as myself, unless they were completely crazy. Yea, I wasn't one of those cats. But does it really matter when I'm one now?

I went back to my cell. The air felt lighter. Weird, it almost felt normal to see them. Killer Mike. Jesus. And Pluto. Nobody knew Pluto's real name. He was borderline psycho, which was good in a way because nobody messed with him. But sometimes he missed it when some cat messed with him, joking around because he was a little slow.

Mike was a white guy in his early 40's. In and out for assault and battery. Kept to himself. While Jesus sometimes got the pronunciation and the spelling of his name mixed up. He was always giving advice when nobody asked him for it. It's a quiet atmosphere after anyone had a visitor. If it was somebody you wanted to see, you felt sad. If it was your lawyer…and you weren't getting out anytime soon, well, you felt even worse. We don't eat popcorn and ice cream in the rec room on that dilapidated sofa. There's little to no cheering when the bad guy gets killed before the commercial break. We don't get to turn off the set. We get told when to go to sleep. And when to wake up.

Cellmates. Before Killer Mike, there was this Indian cat named Taj. I remember the day Taj was released he gave me his old bent up on the edges wall calendar. "Morris, you're alright, I hope I never see you in this place again."

The baton had been passed. I stared at the calendar, then tacked it back up on the wall next to my bed. The next day, I started markin' off the days…just like he used to do.

"How many days you think you'll be here?" Mike asked me

lmost chuckling.

"Don't know."

"What do you weigh?"

"Huh?" I looked confused.

"175."

"Yea," Mike grinned, "That's about right." He and Jesus apped knuckles and laughed a minute.

"Yea, you'll be here about five-and-a-half months...almost 75 days."

The AC was always going out. I know what you're hinkin'...why should they provide air conditioning to inmates? Nell, inside it's more like survival. I remember once. It must've been 100 degrees outside, so the cells felt like hot coals immering inside a barbeque pit. These fools decide to protest. n jail, protesting, exercising our rights, imagine that.

I could hear distant yelling, after about ten minutes, it urned into a roar. The whole ward. Jumpin' up and down, oundin' on the cell bars, throwin' toilet paper. Like something out of a movie. And then somebody down the hallway decided o start a fire. The alarm went off and so did the sprinklers. The nmates cheered!

The correctional officers came runnin' in riot gear like they were gonna shoot us. But they're commanding officer told hem to stand down. We were on lockdown for two weeks. But by then the air conditioner was fixed and everybody let up on hatin' everybody else, things got back to normal. Normal for ail that is.

ALTHEA JEWEL

FOURTEEN

If it's true what they say about leadin' a horse to water. I wasn't ready to give up, I wasn't ready to drink. After all was said and done…I still wanted to maintain custody of my son. The truth was right in front of me but I didn't want to see. I was innocent. I wasn't gonna be bullied by those Whitfield thugs.

Once a week we got to go outside on the yard. It was a dreary extension of what was inside but I could feel real air, look up and see the sky, and if I was lucky a bird might fly overhead, teasing me with what I couldn't be today, free.

They'd let out a dozen or so of us at a time. We stretched out, used the old work out equipment and got a chance to shoot around on a couple basketball hoops. It still felt like fun, even the broken strings on the hoops didn't bother me. Neither did the concrete with uneven patches of dead grass at the free throw line…it wasn't meant to be the local Y. We didn't have basketball shoes anyway…so it didn't matter. Just an hour outside. We knew what we signed up for.

Across the yard was a couple rows of chippy lookin' bleachers. I don't know what the original purpose was for but that's where the gang members congregated. They kicked back shootin' the breeze, seemed harmless, but for all I knew they were just plotting their next move. I kept my distance.

"Yo Holmes," some random guy came over to me while I was shootin' free throws.

I kept bouncin' the ball and stared him down. "The names Morris."

"Ha, you got heart, no disrespect Morris, that's just a friendly way to say what's up."

"Just mindin' mines," I answered him, the ball slid through the hoop. I went to retrieve it.

He kept talkin', "Naw I get it. You short timers, you just wanna get the fuck outta here." I didn't reply. Just went back to my spot and took another free throw.

"You got it," I said without smiling. Then they called our group to go back to our cells. Believe it or not, I learned a lot while I was in there. I had conversations with my cell mates.

"Morris here thinks the world is flat." The other two guys in my cell chuckled. One sat up on his bunk and started in on me. We had been having a discussion about life in general. I was tryin' to plead my case about how the system works. I thought I knew what I was talking about until he stopped me with that world is flat comment.

"Now listen up Morris. I'm gonna hip you to the game… just call me a cosigner."

"Okay," I replied, "Speak on it."

"Why you think so many Black and Brown men are locked up?"

And then he broke down the math. Cases = Job security + supervisor Job security = Us locked down. He laughed and added, "We just pawns in the game, don't you ever forget it."

I began to look at everything from a different perspective. All my life I'd thought that jail kept bad people off the streets. Yes, there are some people who shouldn't be on the outside. But what about all the other people? Deep down I knew he was right. But at that time in my life, even when it was staring me in the face, I didn't want to believe it. We are programmed to not believe the minority. Trust the majority. Expect only good outcomes even in the worst situations. The man is going to come through for us, save us from ourselves if you will.

"Reform us?" he laughed again...his laughter echoed through the hallway.

The next day we learned that some young cat overdosed in his cell. He was on heroin. That really bothered me. Cats have just as much access to drugs on the inside as they do on the streets. Talk about hypocrisy.

We were supposed to be in here to get rehabilitated. But everybody was doing the most behind these walls. And the people that were paid to watch over us just turned a blind eye.

"That's the fifth overdose this month." I couldn't shake the feeling. Even the drugs had been dipped into and circulated back onto the street and smuggled inside here to annihilate more people. "How do drugs get back in here?"

"Naw Morris, you don't want to get into that mindset...just know that it's for real."

"I was just talking out loud man, I really don't have any interest in that type of shit." My patience wore thinner over the next few weeks. Since I'd decided to plead not guilty, it didn't seem like my day in court was coming anytime soon. I reached out to my lawyer once a week. It was always the same thing. Continuance.

By mid-October I started to feel less hopeful that I was going to even beat this thing. Marvin had plead guilty and was awaiting sentencing. And since I was in the car with him, there was no guarantee that I wouldn't be dragged down to the dungeon with him. Especially when he kept to his lie that I was the orchestrator of the whole thing.

But I was innocent. And I thought I had the truth on my side. A week before I was scheduled to appear, my mother came to visit me. I was happy and sad all at the same time. She was wearing a burgundy velour jogging suit, it looked brand new. I complimented her.

"Ma you look great! That material works on you."

Ma smiled and said, "You always know what to say, how are you Curtis?"

I chuckled, "Like pops always said, I've seen better days."

Ma didn't smile when I said that. In fact, I was bracing for a lecture that never came. I had grown a beard but my afro was looking tight. I tugged at my beard nervously. Ma noticed but didn't comment on my new found appearance.

"Your Uncle Joey said for me to tell you don't worry, everything's under control."

"He said that, really?"

"Yes, really. And Lorraine is looking after your children. She's moved into your guest room."

"What about my housekeeper, Mrs. Johnson?"

"Oh, Mrs. Johnson's got a lot to straighten out at her own ouse."

I looked shocked, when Ma said, "Her husband passed way in June."

"Aww Ma, that's terrible," I held my head down for a ninute.

"She has relatives looking after her. Strange. As they tell it, ѥ was fine one day and gone the next."

"Oh Ma, no…that's messed up."

"We went to the funeral. She doesn't need any money. He eft her a fine house."

"Did you tell her about me?"

"No Curtis, I couldn't, I know she is fond of you and asmine…and loved your children."

"Ma, how's Jasmine?"

My mother looked me in the eyes through the glass divider ınd choked back her tears. "I wanted your father to tell you his…but nobody wants to tell you while you're in here."

"Please don't cry Ma…I can't hold it together if you cry on ne now." Ma wouldn't cry. She knew how to cover her tears… ɔut came the laughter.

"Your Uncle has been a good influence on you. But he's not ɔne to take his own advice."

"What?"

"Before you moved to Atlanta, your father and your uncle had a big argument…we didn't really want you to live out there…we were afraid he'd go back to his old ways."

"Ma, please, just say it."

"Curtis, who controls the finances, or are you joint owners?"

"Uncle Joey always has done right by me… he's taking care of my house while I'm in here."

"Well, that may be true. But his wife called and said he's lost over $300,000…gambling."

"Lorraine said he's not drinking but he's got to get help or she's going to put him out."

"I guess I've been gone too long."

"Not by choice," she said in a low voice.

"Ma, Jazz and I are having problems too, I'd rather keep th news between us."

"I've called her a few times just to check on the children. I don't discuss what's going on with the finances with Jasmine."

"Good. Okay, I'm gonna get out of here and make everything alright, please Ma, stop crying, I can't hold it together if I see you cry." She wiped her eyes quickly and composed herself to hear what I was about to say.

"Uncle Joey opened the door for me. And even if he took a fall, I can still make good on my investment."

"So, you're going back there?" she sounded surprised.

"I can't stay here. They'll do something shady again to get me locked back up."

"We can get a good lawyer."

"Naw Ma, I know now, that's not how things work in here, not for people like us."

Before Ma visited me, I thought that pleading my innocence, somehow could change the trajectory of my life. But if I was being honest, really honest, my path was already in front of me, long before I ever got into that truck with Marvin Whitfield.

Of course, the jail system's timin' didn't coordinate with my wake up to reality. I would never suggest that anyone else do what I did. Eight weeks later, they called me back to court and I told Mr. Willoughby I didn't wanna fight, I took the plea deal. They released me in December.

"Son-of-a-bitch, Morris don't you EVER come back up in here," my cellmate chuckled.

"I won't say never, but I sure as hell don't want to see this place again." I put on my wrinkled jacket and caught the first city bus heading towards Cerritos.

ALTHEA JEWEL

FIFTEEN

A light rain drizzled. Another reason to smile. Some people like rain. They say it's a blessing. That's supposed to be like a prayer of protection. I smiled thinking to myself, Allah-u-Akbar, better late than never. An hour and a half later I reached my father's house. The front door was unlocked. I turned the knob and walked inside, locked the door and the top lock.

"Ma, you need to start lockin' this front door," I yelled. "It's a whole different world out there." She ran to greet me, arms outstretched, and hugged me like I was her baby again. I finally got the courage to dial my house, it rang twice before she picked up.

"Jazz, I swear to you, I wasn't involved...I didn't ask for any of this." I set down my sandwich, picked up the cordless phone, and walked to the back of my parent's house.

"Curtis, I can't believe how irresponsible you are, it's been eight months!!!" She always made it sound like I asked for something awful to happen.

"They wanted to give me eight years!!!"

She yelled back, "I KEEP TELLING YOU, put ME, US, YOUR FAMILY FIRST!"

Pay real close attention. Whoever the next woman is, always subconsciously and sometimes intentionally, tries to compare her relationship with you, with your ex. Your first baby mama is supposed to walk ten feet behind your current wife, 2nd mama five feet, 3rd mama one foot, you follow me?

"Jasmine, damn! I got locked up tryin' to bring OUR son home…I thought he was your son too?"

"Here we go again, what else Jazz, huh, like that movie… cut my hand off for you?"

"See, that's what I'm talking about, you are SO disrespectful, I'm done." Did she just say that she's done?

"Huh?...What?" She might as well have spat out the word nigga in front of repeating my words back to me.

She said it with some backbone to it, "Huh? What? You heard me."

I dropped my shoulders. "I kept hearing while I was locked up that you would leave me…now that I'm out, I see for myself…and how long you been sleeping around?" She was quiet. I could hear the baby fidgeting in the background. That must've hit a nerve.

She had the audacity to hang the phone up. But she never admitted to cheating on me. As crazy as it sounds, the past eight months gave me a break from a broken relationship. Things weren't cool between us before this whole jail fiasco. So busy workin' and contemplatin' getting Aaron back, that maybe she felt I was neglecting her. But I thought that I was doing what I was supposed to do. The next call I made was to my Uncle Joey.

"Uncle Joey!"

"Curtis! Man, when you coming home?" I didn't know if I should greet him or punch his lights out.

"I'll be taking the train home tomorrow. Can you pick me up from the station?"

"Yes, let me know what time and I'll come getcha."

"Thank you. And thank you and auntie for helpin' out while I was gone."

You know. It's funny. I thought I was a decent guy with a good head on my shoulders. But I was ignorant to how far people are willing to go. I imagined Mrs. Parker, the mediator in our custody hearing saying, "As long as you're not endangering Aaron you will maintain joint custody," and at that exact moment I remembered that look in Bernard Whitfield's eyes. He'd found a way to make me look like I could somehow endanger my son. Now I have a criminal record. That's all it took.

A few days later I arrived back home in Georgia. My uncle wasn't his usual self, didn't talk much. Half-smiled. He dropped me off in front of my house and nodded, "Call me."

Whatever it was he couldn't say that day…he'd tell me later. I'd been sensing somethin' was wrong, even before I could put my key in the door. Maryam was standing in the foyer, visibly shaken up. I didn't say anything. Just smiled and gave her a big hug.

I took notice, the curtains had been removed. Screws lifted and tiny holes remained in place of the artwork. Furniture scrapes on my walls. Bookcase emptied out, except for my Holy Quran, wrapped in a white linen cloth, practically the

only thing left as I'd left it. I walked slowly towards the kitchen
Cabinets with handles loose, left wide open. Jazz was leaving
without even saying goodbye.

My voice cracked as I asked Maryam, "Where's your
mother?" She hesitated. I opened the refrigerator. Practically
empty.

"Gettin' another van with the movers," she finally answered

"How long you been moving?" I opened a can of soda and
halfway grinned.

"About three days."

I nodded, looked at her sad face, "Yea, a lot is different
here."

"Yeah, yesterday they picked up your dogs."

"What?"

"Yeah, the dogs are at grandpa's now."

I held my head down and asked God to give me strength. I
noticed all the photos of my kids were removed from outside
the fridge.

"Where are your sisters?" Just then the moving truck pulled
up in my driveway and I heard Jasmine giving instructions.
I turned to walk towards the front door. "You wait here
Maryam."

I don't think Jazz was expecting me until tomorrow. But
I got back a lot quicker. The plan was to be gone before I got
here. Well damn, okay, I'm just gonna act cool and play my
part.

"Let me help you with that Jazz," I worked alongside her
workers organizing the moving truck. She blinked her eyes and
pretended not to notice my non-resistance.

"Curtis, she said softly towards time to leave, "I didn't want...."

I cut her off, "I guess my daughters and my dogs are at your father's house?"

I gently pulled her arm before she could walk away, "After all we've been through?" The dining room was completely ghost. The table was still there. But four chairs were missing. I guess she figured I couldn't sit down on more than one chair at a time.

Maryam was crying. "Mama, I don't want to move."

Holdin' onto me for dear life. "I don't wanna live in California."

Jasmine tried to calm her down. "Maryam, we talked about this...what about your sisters?" Then they walked into the hallway, whispering.

"But I've already sent your things to grandpa's house, your clothes, your shoes, everything." Wow. What kind of woman takes a man's children...his furniture...and his dogs? That was how things ended between me and my soon-to-be-ex-wife. I found a big bag of potato chips and pulled a cold soda out the fridge and sat on my front porch.

The sky was threatening rain. I watched the sunset and waited for the night to fall. It had all happened so fast. For the best, I'd told myself, but I knew better. It's been documented how encouraging the separation of Black and minority families destroys the unit of future generations. Breaks down the unit. Keeps single moms on welfare. Puts single dads in the penitentiary.

The next day I slept. I let go of all that bad energy. And the following day, I slept some more. On day three...I woke up to the sounds of crows in the distance behind my back yard. I got up, shaved, showered, made myself some breakfast, and went back to work. Staying busy kept me anchored. There was a gaping hole in my marriage boat. I get it, preachers, Imams, counselors say just keep fighting and patch it up. I wasn't one to believe in fixing structural issues...eventually that hole comes back. And, it gets bigger and bigger and bigger, until one day, the boat tips over... and it's sinking...

A month or so later, I was in the kitchen, my auntie stopped by while I was puttin' groceries away.

"Curtis, you weren't gone long enough to make her leave... her mind was made up way before that."

"Yea, auntie, but you know people judge."

"People judge. But your family shouldn't."

I sat back down at the table. "Yea, you're right. I guess she just wanted out."

"You want some turkey sausage and grits?"

"No," she said, "Sounds good but I just came over to see how you're getting along." She got the coffee maker out and made a fresh pot. I cooked, finished my meal and rinsed out my plate, she'd already cleared the pans from the stove.

"I can order some curtains for you for the front two rooms...I just need to know what kind of material you like."

"Aww auntie, thank you...ceiling to floor like the last ones."

We looked at the windows in the living room. "But a little more sheer...like a fancy hotel."

"Fancy hotel?" she laughed, "Who you bringing up in here?"

"Nobody yet," I grinned with a little embarrassment.

She changed the subject. "The curtains, you want beige, or yellow to match the walls?"

"No, let's paint the walls a new color, any color than what they are."

"Okay, we can just make the curtains sheer, matches everything."

"Yea, I like that," I said in agreement. I got my ladder from my truck so we could take measurements. My aunt had something else on her mind. She didn't hesitate to have her say.

"I know you've heard about your Uncle Joey. He's not doing so good."

I climbed up on the ladder, "Been rough lately."

"I'm so sorry Curtis. Contractors came to me and said he was losin' a lot of money…it's not going to be easy to salvage the business."

"You don't have to explain auntie, I'll find a way."

"You know, he had a big argument with your wife Jasmine about it."

"What?"

"Yea, she figured out what was going on and confronted him."

"How did she find out?"

"Your uncle drove over to your house."

"Checking on the kids?"

"No, he was desperate for money. Gambling. I told him I was done with all that." I scribbled some notes down on the notepad, then looked back at auntie.

"He thought he could ask your wife for a loan."

"Is that why Jasmine left me?"

"No, that's not why, you mean she didn't tell you what happened?" Turns out, Jasmine was seeing somebody else. When Joey showed up, another man answered my door, no shirt on…and pajama pants.

"I knew Jazz was unhappy. But I didn't think she'd bring another man into my house." As if things couldn't get any worse, I learned from my attorney, Mr. Willoughby, my visitation was on hold because Allison had filed a restraining order.

"Are you kidding me?"

"No, apparently she is doing all she can to keep you away."

"But I pay child support and I have rights, don't I?" Right when he told me the bad news, I happened to be cleaning my gun. I set it down on the nightstand, wiped my hand across my forehead, and sat on the edge of my bed.

"Curtis, I'm sorry." And then he paused, "I was pushing to get some way around it." I tugged at my goatee and kept listening.

"I was banking on your household being more stable. But with you and your wife separating, that kills the logic." I looked at the rifle and my eyebrow twitched.

"Unstable? Really? Maybe I should just blow my brains out, what do you think counselor?"

"What are you talking about?" he sounded stunned.

I felt my heart racing. "Man, I'm sitting here, right now, cleanin' my gun, I'm not suicidal but I'm thinking, maybe God would forgive me, for how I want to shoot somebody…thank God I don't live in California!"

"Curtis, don't talk like that. You have to be level headed. Get in a social setting and don't be isolating yourself…I know a good therapist in your city, I'll give him a call."

"That won't be necessary, I'm not going to shoot anybody, I'm just tired of all this bullshit." After we said goodbye, I stood in the mirror over my bedroom dresser and posed. It was stupid. For a brief moment I held back being so poised and disciplined. I looked at my reflection, imagined a predator dead on the floor beneath me. And then I caught hold of my darker thoughts, carefully set the gun down on my dresser and poured out the bullets. It was 2:00 in the afternoon. Early by all accounts. But close to being late enough to call it a day.

"Aww, a beauty!" the gun shop owner said, admiring the gun he'd just bought back from me.

"Yep, I took good care of her," I said with a half-grin. Like a pawn shop, he cut the price, handed me a receipt and three-hundred dollars.

"Anything else I can do for you Curtis?"

"No Henry, I'm good. Take care."

"You do the same."

ALTHEA JEWEL

SIXTEEN

Every day felt like an out-of-body experience, my marriage was over. Now, I wasn't seeing any of my kids. That's just the way it was. Maryam, now 12, called, every Sunday. She kept me well-informed about the ups and downs livin' with her grandparents.

"Mama wants to talk with you."

"Ask her what she wants," I'd always say, it was easier just to get the point. Let me say for the record, reconciling is doable for a lot of cats. I'm a firm believer, and you don't have to agree with me, but your ex is an ex for a reason. Sure, that picturesque relationship is every man's fantasy.

Everybody wants a do over. Everybody wants to sugar-coat it and "just accept" their partner's flaws. But I'm not everybody. I'm not even the 3% that I call the realist. I'm somewhere in the ten to twenty percent who know that life, love, relationships are complicated. But I don't want to be shackled or handcuffed to be with anyone. Truth be told, I was happiest when I was a kid, runnin' track with my sister in Cerritos. That special time has never been recaptured or duplicated. The age of innocence.

I don't want time to stand still. I don't want to be a kid again. But I sure miss being, feeling, and living…on top of the world.

People say, just do whatever it takes, for the sake of your children. That's how I got here. But just like how I'm here, I don't want to go back. I don't want to be with Allison or Jasmine. The age after innocence. The age of reality check. If going back means losing all over again, I don't think my heart, my mind, nor my soul could recover from that. No, no regrets, and I know what's expected of me. And I vowed to myself, no matter what, to always take care of my children. A month or so later, I found myself faced with: How can I keep that promise?

"Ah hello, good morning, I'm Curtis Morris, here to apply for the construction job." Every time I introduce myself to corporate America, it leaves a bad taste in my mouth. Before the internet you had to find a job in the newspaper. You had to get dressed. Gas up your vehicle and drive to a building, check a list of jobs posted behind a glass bookcase. You'd read through the list and go inside a room, glance up at the clock, always facing you to remind you of that "time is of the essence" bullshit and smile a big cheesecake grin.

I remember walkin' up to that check-in table wearing a crisp dress shirt and a dark blue tie. There was a room full of men and a couple chicks hovering over their clipboards, writing in uniformed silence. I found an empty desk, cleared my throat, sat down and started writing: Full name, birthdate, social security number, home address, marital status, who do they contact in case of emergency. It felt so intrusive. But if you want the job, you better be prepared and willing to fill in every blank.

And, after that general question section, then the real question: Have you ever been convicted of a felony? It was a knee jerk reaction. They make it sound so dirty. Felony. I held my pen up and flipped through the application to see how much more they wanted to know. Then I waited a minute flipped back to the next question and stared like I wanted the page to burn from my gaze...but it didn't. It read clearly: Are you on probation? I waited about a minute before I got up from my seat, and approached the lady at the front desk.

"Excuse me," I said almost in a whisper to the receptionist.

She looked up batting her eyelashes and said, "Yes, may I help you?"

"I didn't bring my references. Can I take this application back home, complete it..."

She cut me off, "Yes, sure just bring everything back... we're open until 5." I looked up at the clock on the wall, ticking loudly, close to eleven o'clock. I gathered my papers up, the metal legs on the chair scraped the floor and I left. Later never came. After recouping my confidence, I ventured out later that week. I came across an ad for a commercial painter. Someone to travel to local businesses and paint walls. How hard could that be? Decent pay with no overhead. They're application didn't ask about the background check, but I had something else working against me.

Mistake number one: I was counting the money before it was in my pocket. After I carefully filled out the app, I smiled and waited to be interviewed. They were hiring multiple people. For sure, one of those spots had to have my name on it. Come on, it's gotta be today!

I sat patiently. The door opened, from the inside hallway, two cats, both Hispanic, and a white guy, came out smiling, both hired on the spot. But me? It wasn't happening.

I asked politely, "How long will my application be on file?" An older white cat shuffling papers, then reached to answer a phone line grinned, "Up to one year." I realized it was going to be challenging working for somebody else when I had owned my own business. But my attitude was different. $5 more than zero was something. The longer you go without making money the longer it takes to pay off monies owed in the rears. I don't know how else to live…so I looked Monday through Friday.

My family loves camping and my Uncle Joey loved fishing. He asked me to go one Saturday, early, up to Lake Lanier. Clean fresh air. Beautiful rocky landscape. A piece of heaven on earth.

"I love it here," I said thankfully, "I'm glad you wanted to take a break."

Uncle Joey lowered his line in the water. "Yep, nothing like nature."

Another boat passed. We tossed our poles and waited on bass for the next several hours. By noon Joey had caught a few. My line was still empty but it was still considered early. Looking back, I'm glad we didn't speak about his gambling problem. It must've not been that bad, he hadn't lost his wife or his house. We all have vices. That day, was kinda strange, every fish he caught, he'd reel in, then let them off the hook, and throw them back into the water.

After about five fish, I asked him, "Why you throwin' them back, they not big enough?"

"Hahahaha, Curtis, always the joker... you know your grand-father was just like you." And then he told me a story about how my grandpa used to do this magic trick.

"He would tell you to look away, and before you could look back, he'd pull this round wooden circle the size of a nickel, seemed to come out of your ear...but you never felt anything."

"Oh, I remember, grandpa and his wooden nickel jokes."

"Yea, he was a good man. Grew up when marrying outside our race got you killed." Me and pops definitely didn't look biracial. Uncle Joey was a carmel-brown complexion, but in the winter his skin looked much lighter. I guess the Canadian ancestry had skipped a generation. My sister Waleena was fair-skinned. And now, my daughter, Naomi was fairer than the rest of my children. We all considered ourselves Black. I wondered if Naomi will someday want to be tanned, darker, the way my sister used to want to.

I also remember my pops saying, "They tried to burn grandpa's house down to the ground!" My grandparents left North Carolina and settled in New York, lived out their lives and were buried there.

I asked my uncle, "You ever think about moving back to North Carolina?" He nodded yes as he reeled in a fish and inspected it.

"A good one, four, maybe five pounds," he lifted it, then tossed it back into the lake.

"North Carolina, beautiful. Marry who you want. They don't like it much, but they ain't killing over it." He went on, "Did your dad ever tell you about the land?" Surprised, I shook my head no.

"About two-and-a-half acres of prime real estate, it's been empty all these years. But now I think it's worth going back for." And that was the only good news.

"Oh, you're going back?" I said with a big smile.

SEVENTEEN

"No, I don't have the energy. But Curtis, you're still young…my time is running out." A larger boat seemed to disappear in the distance.

"The house here belongs to Lorraine. We had a good life. Shared it all…even the bad."

"Yea, Uncle J, you two make a good team."

"I didn't do right by you Curtis, you've always been good, like a son to me."

I didn't want him to put himself down. I just said, "Shit happens."

"Yea, shit does, agree with you on that." He went on to say, "The land, I put the deed in your name, it's yours Curtis…to keep in the family." Wait a minute, I asked myself, why is he saying all this.

"Curtis, I'm 49, almost 50 years. Made it halfway, I guess that's just my portion." It sounded so final. I pulled my fishing line back into the boat.

"What are you saying, Uncle Joey?"

He took a long breath. His jawbone clenched a little and then he said it, "I've got cancer."

I set my fishing pole down and processed the bad news. On the ride back home, my mind was racing. From the time I'd moved to Atlanta, up to this very moment. I sat next to him in his truck, silently, while we pulled the boat back to the house.

We got almost to his driveway, he said, "Auntie wants chemo for me…I haven't decided on that yet."

It turns out they didn't want chemotherapy. They opted for home care. Uncle Joey's den was converted into a semi-hospital room. The doctor set up an IV drip with morphine and a nurse stayed in their guest room, five days and nights, weekly to care for him. She was off Tuesday and Wednesday.

We visited in rotation. My folks came down from California and a half-dozen or so of Aunt Lorraine's relatives, along with their pastor; slept, ate, and prayed around the clock for over six weeks.

"Curtis, he wants to see you," Aunt Lorraine's eyes puffy with tears. I walked in, the curtains were drawn, not much light coming in from the outside. I glanced at a vase, filled with fresh water and bright yellow sunflowers. He watched, as I sat next to his bed. My chair squeaked as I forced my body to be still. And even though I wasn't in a hospital room, I was.

"Hey buddy," he said and smiled, "I thought I fixed that chair…guess we just have to replace it."

"Naw," I shook my head, "Chair's fine." Dark circles around his eyes, he'd lost a lot of weight. But he was shaven and alarmingly calm.

"Curtis, I need to ask you something."

"Sure, anything."

"After I…," and he stopped then continued, "After I'm gone, I don't want Lorraine to be alone." I leaned in closer and put my hand on his shoulder.

"Get her out to my brother's house, your father's house in California."

"Sure thing, I can do that. Anything else?"

"Yea, make sure you take my boat with you to North Carolina."

I smiled, "I'd be happy to do that, maybe even catch some fish sometimes."

"Maybe so," he smiled, he knew I wasn't good at fishing. Even though I knew it was going to be one of our last conversations, I knew how much I meant to him, and that I mattered.

Two nights later, Uncle Joey took his last breaths. It was summer. 1990. Aunt Lorraine wanted a funeral but my parents talked her into a memorial instead.

"Salaams Kareem, sorry to hear about your uncle's passing."

"Yea, he was like a father to me, thank you Ahmad." I was helping my aunt go through a lot of financial paperwork, a stack covering my dining room table.

He went on to say, "And how are you doing out there in that house since the divorce?"

"Me? Busy, helping my auntie and working."

He went silent for a moment, then asked me, "Are you in touch with your Imam?"

I almost stuttered, "No, I ah ah…haven't been to the masjic in a while." I was half-listening to him, he meant well but I wasn't in that space anymore. While he was talking, I was thinking about yesterday, I'd sprinkled some fertilizer on my brown grass.

There was a brief pause. "Kareem, I know you, thinking about something else to tune me out." I breathed in the smell from my back yard, oddly, it didn't bother me.

"Yeah, Ahmad, no need to worry about me, I'm just getting the house in order."

I went on to say, "Can I be honest?"

"Yes, my brother, speak freely."

"After Alee, Jasmine stole my heart. We married in Islam. Now, I'm reminded of how bad, good intentions can be. I feel blindsided, tainted by my choice to follow religion."

"Don't leave now, we need strong brothers like you, to teach the younger ones."

"That may well be, but I'm taking a neutral path. I will always be a Muslim. But I'm stepping off the mountain, at least for now."

"That's your choice. Free will. Return when you're ready. Insha Allah."

"Insha Allah," I replied.

Ahmad changed the subject, "So what happens to the business?"

"Aww man, we closed it down."

"Why don't you start back up on the west coast?"

RIDICULE

I closed my screen door then locked the latch. I laughed,
"That's not an option."

"Didn't you hear what happened?"

"Hear what?"

ALTHEA JEWEL

EIGHTEEN

"Marvin Whitfield got arrested."

"Doesn't change anything for me, the damage is already done."

"Yea, but he's getting his due, for the awful thing he put you through."

"See, I don't agree with that," I said sternly.

I went on to say, "People do crazy shit to other people all the time, and it doesn't always come back to haunt them."

I sold the home I'd built for my wife and children and sent Jasmine's divorce papers to my attorney. The same time I moved to Charlotte was the same time I got off probation. I saw a parallel between the two. I guess it was physical and emotional freedom. Don't get me wrong. As you know, I'm not perfect. My deeds will never be forgotten. But I seek refuge. Forgiveness.

I remember plannin' to sell the house. I was gathering everything, what to keep and what to toss. Maybe I should've never held on so long. Letters. Memos. Cards. Pictures of Jasmine, my Muslim queen. Those memories wrapped in twine. I tossed all but one, the one when she was pregnant with our first child. The rest went into the fireplace and I lit the match.

Looking back, I guess you could say that I loved strong. And that was my downfall. I swore before Jehovah, God, and Allah that it would not be my legacy. North Carolina, she rescued me. North Carolina has good bones and diversity. It's beautiful gardens, future homes of the best arenas, halls and universities. Like Duke and the University of North Carolina at Chapel Hill.

I embraced the hills and the history. Impressed by the acknowledgment of Black cultural exhibits and centers. In awe that the city was named after King George III's wife, Queen Charlotte. I would've preferred a namesake after my own people...as we know the land was stolen and was built up by slaves. Again, refuge. Forgiveness. That's why I love Charlotte.

Settling in was pretty smooth. I found a nice apartment, small unit, on a street lined with young Sycamore trees. I had a little patio where I could smoke my pipe and watch the awesome sunset. There were only four units. I met the woman who lived downstairs from me, a nice retired lady, with her small dog. A Shih Tzu. She held it under her arm, like a baby. I never saw that dog's feet on the ground. She'd wave from her picturesque window and I'd wave back and smile. Whenever I'd see her unloading her car, I'd always help her with her groceries, she loved to shop.

"Thank you so much." Her name was Elizabeth Craig. It wasn't polite to ask, but she was probably in her late sixties. Her husband had died five years ago. She was very independent and opinionated...most of the time.

"Mrs. Craig, anything else you need?" Her long gray hair was pulled back in a pony tail. She kept it braided.

"Oh, Curtis, you're the best, can I pay you something for helping me?"

"No ma'am, anytime I'm around, just let me know."

On the way out of her apartment I noticed the paint on her walls was chippy and peeling. I thought to call the landlord. Then I just asked Mrs. Craig if she'd mind me painting her kitchen.

"Here Curtis," she tried to shove money in my hand, and I set it down on her countertop.

"Ma'am," I said quietly.

"I know, I know, you won't take any money, I'm not that old, I'm 72 years young."

"Wow Miss Craig, you really look much younger."

"Aww thank you Curtis, you're such a polite young man." I kept busy for a few months. Working my day job, and finding some guys to put a fence around the westside of my new property. It was time to meet with the contractors and developers to come up with the right building plans.

Back in California, Naomi, my youngest, started kindergarten. Her mom sent me a bunch of photos of the kids. They were all growing up too fast. Jazz sent me a photo of herself, lounging outside by her parent's swimming pool. I placed her picture face down on the coffee table, picked up the newspaper and then the telephone rang.

"Hello, Curtis, just wanted to hear your voice."

"Auntie! How's Hawaii?"

"Just wonderful, your mother and I just coming from dinner and a show." Pops doesn't like traveling and the altitude on the plane affected his blood pressure.

"Have you moved onto the land yet?"

"No, just getting the fence around it…haven't even got the plans drawn up just yet."

"Hold on a minute, Claudia!"

"Hello sweetheart."

"Hi Ma! Enjoying your vacation?" I stopped browsing through the paper and smiled to hear their excitement.

"Oh Curtis, this place is so beautiful, you need to take a vacation."

"Yea Ma, I will someday soon."

"How's pops doing at the house by himself?"

"He's doing okay. We left him with a refrigerator full of food and beer."

"Hahaha," I laughed, "He's all set then."

"This call is costing him, so I'll say goodbye for now… Aloha!"

"Cool Ma, Aloha."

I had two weeks off just before the new year. I thought maybe I could see my kids at my folks. Turns out, Jasmine's father had started a Christmas tradition, they would all be in Hawaii, of all places, until after January 4th the day I went back to work.

NINETEEN

It was 1993. I was almost thirty-years-old and hadn't been reunited with any of my children. Still shell-shocked about my short but painful chapter with the judicial system.

If Mr. Whitfield wanted me to stay out of California, he may have very well gotten his wish. I stayed in Charlotte. I kept to myself. I worked. Paid my bills. And met my obligations. After I'd sanded and painted Mrs. Craig's apartment, she got inspired and redecorated. Turns out her husband was a carpenter. He'd built a lot of her furniture. She kept some of the pieces he'd made but replaced most of them so the house would feel new.

She reflected, "I always thought I'd be the first to leave this earth."

I admired the carved wooden frame around the guest bath mirror, looked custom. "Well, you women seem to always live longer," I laughed.

"My goodness," she chuckled, "I guess we drive you to the grave first, huh?"

"No ma'am I didn't mean it like that."

"I know Curtis, I was just kidding."

Jasmine only called me when she needed something. Usually something she'd messed up and she wanted me to fix it. This time, it wasn't any different. But this time, I wanted the call.

"Jazz, just send her here, I'll take care of her."

"Can she come by herself?" Damn I thought, what happened to the maternal instinct. Maryam, from her recent pictures, had skipped the teenage years and had matured much more than the typical fifteen-year-old girl.

"Okay Curtis, I'll send her, I'm done trying…maybe you can straighten her out."

"I don't know what you mean by that Jazz, I always want to see my children."

"Well," Jasmine insisted, "She missed summer school, so just make sure she stays busy."

Looking back, I was upset that my daughter wasn't getting along with her mother. People always ask the same dumb question, "Well how close were they?" Or say something like, "They weren't close."

And I'm baffled. What do they mean by that? What difference does that make, when a woman births a child into the world, they are connected, by umbilical cord. How much closer can they get? I was secretly hoping Maryam would have to stay with me. At least through college. It was a warm afternoon. Her flight was on time. Half the plane exited and there she stood.

"Maryam!" We ran towards each other and I spun her around. We hugged and cried for what felt like five minutes.

Five minutes is a long time for a grown man to stand in a public place and cry.

"Wow Maryam, look how grown up you are," I said wiping both our tears.

"You look different too," she grinned.

I was cognizant that maybe the stress had aged me. "Yes," I laughed, "Daddy is getting older too."

But I was right, she didn't look fifteen. The first thing I noticed was her clothes. Baggy jeans, long white T-shirt, and her hair stuffed underneath a UCLA baseball cap. I thought, maybe this dress code was just a way for her to get some attention. She insisting on carting her own luggage. Same ole' Maryam.

"You hungry?" I asked revving the truck engine.

"A little bit."

"I cooked your favorite tonight, roasted chicken and mashed potatoes," I said proudly. She nodded, acknowledging my preparing for her. I rolled down my window and started driving, then turned down the volume on my radio. Maryam finally began to look relaxed in the passenger seat. She yawned, then sat back. It was a relief to accomplish just gettin' one of my children…it was a huge blessing.

I thanked God for that day. I asked her, "Do you remember when you first met me?"

She laughed, "Yeah, you drove us home from school."

"Uh huh, your mother wanted to introduce us but she was nervous."

She cracked her window, laughing, "Mama never knows what to say."

I nodded in agreement but made no comment about it. I laughed heartily, "And you squinted your eyes at me the whole ride."

"I'd never seen you before, I was checking you out."

"Yea, you were very protective of your mother, as you should be." I put my blinker on to get on the freeway, checkin' my mirror.

"Look what it got me!" she shot back.

I didn't respond. I decided long ago, that if I ever got to see my children, I wouldn't speak negatively of their mother. Even if she'd poisoned them from me. We drove in silence the next half hour and I finally got to the house. It was almost 6:00pm and she was asleep. I didn't have a driveway yet. I tried drivin' over the gravel slow but Maryam woke up.

"Where are we, this isn't our house?"

I drove onto the place where the driveway would soon be, and parked. The landscaped trees and plants enclosed the sides of most of my property.

"This is our new house, you like it?"

"Man," she said, "We're rich now!"

She settled in just fine. It's a four bedroom house, my room upstairs, and she picked the one down the hallway, facing one of the most peaceful views. Nothing but green outside her window. She put her clothes in the washer, showered, fixed her hair, and changed into her pajamas. It was just before 8pm when I announced that dinner was ready. I'd learned how to set a table, by watchin' a program about dining etiquette.

"Dad, you really have it all together, I knew you would."

I bowed my head, "Let's say grace."

"Uh, I dunno…"

"Not the Muslim way…just a way to thank God for our food." I reach over and took her hand.

"God, thank you for bringing my daughter, Maryam home, and for the food that we are about to receive, for the nourishment of our minds and our bodies, Amen."

"Amen," Maryam said softly.

I bought some furniture for this house before I moved in. I wanted my kitchen and my dining room to be on point. Out of all the things I didn't care for about Jasmine, she was right about one thing. A house is only home when family gathers and feels connected. In the dining room. At our round table.

"So, Maryam, my dear, tell me what's been going on?" I don't know if it was just the timing but at that moment, I heard the sound of her utensil, her knife had slipped out of her hand and it made a really loud sound on her plate.

She picked it up quickly, placed it on her napkin. "Sorry," she said, "I guess I'm just tired."

It was a minute or two before I picked up the next conversation. "My Uncle Joey, got me started in the construction business, when I was 17." She smiled politely while eating her food. I went on to say, "About three years ago, he passed away, cancer."

"Oh no, that's awful, how old was your uncle?"

"He was 49…too young."

"Was he in a lot of pain?"

I thought back to the day I was on the boat. Our last time fishing. "If he was, he didn't show it," I said in a low voice.

"Anyway, he left us this land we're on…right now."

"What about the other house, where we lived with Mama?"

"I sold it. Some of the money is put away for you, your sisters, and your big brother Aaron."

"Well," she said, "I guess we shouldn't go back to that house anyway."

"Why?"

"It wouldn't be the same," she said in a sad tone. Maryam normally cleans her plate. Not tonight. She played in the food more than anything.

"You not hungry?" I finally asked.

"No, everything is just how I like it, I'm."

I stopped chewing, "What's wrong Maryam?"

"Daddy I really need to tell you something."

I set my fork down, "Okay."

"Uh, I'm becoming a young adult now," she said almost defiantly.

"A young adult, isn't that just how it is?" My first fear was that she was going to tell me she was pregnant. That would've explained the slouchy baggy pants. Or so I imagined. I became angry just thinkin' about it. Not my child, changing her future before it could even begin. And how dare Jasmine not give me a heads up on this bullshit. But I kept my cool. I shifted into concerned parent mode.

And that's when she said it. "Mama and me don't get along because I'm gay."

My mind drifted back to 1988 when she was 10. I pictured that girl, Regina, from down the street…always walking her dog with Maryam. I suspected something but couldn't put my finger on it.

"Okay," I finally said, "But Mama can't change how you feel, that's for you to decide." Now I understand. I felt like I should

ave protected her when Jazz judged her. I held her like a baby
nd let her cry it out. There wasn't anything else for me to
ay. We spent the next two weeks getting to know each other
ll over again. I took her shopping and bought her clothes,
ats, vests, shoes, and a scooter. She had outgrown dogs and
icycles. Told her that her hair was too pretty to cover up. She
greed to finding a salon to condition and style it for her. I
icked her, and her straightened shoulder length hair, up from
he salon.

"It's a press perm, no chemicals," she quickly told me. She
vas beaming and so happy about it.

"I can wear it like this, then wash it and wear my braids and
fro puffs."

"It looks beautiful, very nice Maryam."

I almost blew it by asking, "So, are you the girl or the guy
girl?"

"It's not that simple," she said defensively.

There was an awkward silence and I said, "I'm sorry, I
lidn't mean to offend you."

"It's a fair question," she replied, "I'm sorry too dad.
overreacted." Later that night she told me that she isn't
nasculine, or even sure about her identity. "I like girls and they
ike me."

I accepted her choice to love who she wants to. I laid down
he same laws for her as I would any other child living under
ny roof. Your friends are welcomed. No sleepin' over. I'm not
oreathin' down your neck 24-7. Maryam and I got along just
ine. Her mother would call and she didn't even want to speak.

"Just talk for a minute, she's your mother, mind your
nanners."

Maryam said, "I have nothing to say."

Jasmine tried to convince me that the riff between them was Maryam's fault. "It doesn't matter Jazz, you're the adult, you have to try to make this right."

"Or what?" By now Maryam had gone upstairs to her room and closed the door.

"I don't know what to tell you, but if you disown her, you'll live to regret it."

TWENTY

That was the last time I spoke with Jasmine about our daughter's lifestyle. In fact, I told her to send the rest of Maryam's things to North Carolina. The packages arrived so soon...she must've been hoping, waiting for me to ask. The 4th of July weekend was coming up. In California there would be a picnic in the park. Not then in North Carolina. Two days before the celebration, bad weather. It wasn't a close call but big news when a plane crashed in some trees near Charlotte airport. 37 people were killed.

Ma called sounding panicky, "Curtis, is everything alright?"

"Yea Ma, that crash is nowhere near here but everybody's on edge... real bad thunderstorm."

"Oh, thank God you're okay. We heard the news and just checking on you."

"We're fine Ma, Maryam, and me, are just fine."

"You know you shouldn't let that girl go back to her mother's house."

I walked over to the thermostat and turned off the heat. Maryam's hands and feet were always cold. I kept it toasty around the house when it felt chilly.

"She's not going back Ma…she's staying right here."

"Okay good. Sweetheart I love you."

"Love you too Ma." A few minutes later I heard Maryam laughing in her room, as usual, on the telephone. I walked past her door, breathed in a sigh of relief. My oldest daughter was home, safe and sound. People think being away from your children must be easy. After all, somebody else is doing all the work. But it's really just the opposite. I had many sleepless nights, alone, waiting, worrying and wondering if I would ever see any of them again. Without me asking, Jasmine mailed me Maryam's school records. Jasmine had done what Allison was never willing to do. Just let it go.

"Okay Maryam, you're enrolled in school. Focus on your grades…don't worry about anything else." She turned a half cartwheel in the middle of our living room. Just a little bit rusty.

"Are you coaching anywhere?"

"No," I chuckled, "But if I get back in shape, rather, if we get back, it might be in the cards."

She found my basketball and started dribbling, "Stop playin' dad, this ball got lots of air in it."

"Okay, I get you…I'll get the yard squared away, put up a hoop again."

"Just a hoop?" she grinned, "You got enough back there to build a full court."

"Hahahahaha," I laughed, "Why do people from California volunteer to spend all my money."

"Dad, I'm not like that, I can get a job."

"Not until you finish college."

"So, I'm staying here with you?"

"As long as you want to."

Time passed quickly with my daughter around. Maryam was becoming a young adult. Her need to express herself with her outward appearance was subtle. She was an athletic girl who just happened to like other athletic girls. She wore expensive looking gear and changed her hairstyle, frequently. She said she was giving her hair a break from straightening. It was freshly washed and in a pony tail.

"Is it okay if I go to the shop to get my hair braided?"

"As long as you've got your work done."

I bought some backyard furniture and a new barbeque pit. I was lounging, looking out over the view, breathing in the fresh air, and contemplating throwing a couple steaks and some corn on the grill.

"I just finished folding and putting away the laundry." You could smell the fabric softener all inside the house.

"Did you mop the kitchen floor?"

"Yes, everything is done."

I smiled, "Yea, okay, then take the truck."

"Thanks dad."

Maryam was a great daughter. Always thoughtful. Whenever she borrowed the truck, she brought it back with more gas in it, even if she only went to the store and back.

"I'm inviting your mother to your graduation." Maryam breathed a stressful sigh. She hadn't seen her mother in over a year.

"I know," I said, "She's never been able to admit when she's wrong."

Maryam's eyes teared up, "I don't even care if she comes or not. I really don't." I knew she cared. Those were angry tears. Her defense mechanism…we've all done it. I still didn't understand my ex. It had to be more to it than homophobia. I was too far away from her to figure it out. We sent Jasmine and family an invite to her eldest daughter's high school graduation.

Two weeks before the ceremony, Maryam said, "She's not coming, is she." It turns out there was more to this story. And I couldn't bear to tell Maryam. Not yet anyway. The night before I was outside on the patio when Jasmine's step-father, Dr. Goldstein called me.

I closed the screen doors and sat on the lounge chair. "Hello Dr. Goldstein."

"Come on Curtis, just call me Larry."

"I take it you aren't coming to the graduation."

He chuckled meekly, "No, there's been a development."

I stood up abruptly and replied nervously, "Development? What does that mean?" I could hear my children's laughter in the background, then his loud footsteps, walking away. I heard a door close and suddenly, all was silent.

"Jasmine hasn't been well, uh, she's…she's in a treatment facility."

"Why?"

"To put it frankly, Curtis, Jasmine had a nervous breakdown."

I was completely off-guard, in shock. "What happened?"

"Well, it's been very difficult since she and the children moved here."

"Difficult? You moved her in to get her away from me!"

"Now, just a minute," he said nervously, "Calm down."

"Okay, I see how you take care of your step daughter, robably was you who sent Maryam's clothes to me, right?"

"Curtis, Jasmine hasn't been well…long before you were 1arried to her."

"Okay, I see, now you pumped her up with prescription rugs, and got her put away, now you're rewriting history and m supposed to just believe your side of the story?"

"I'm sorry, I just wanted to call and tell you how terribly orry we are."

I raised my voice, "Man, just put her mother on the ›hone." After I spoke with Jasmine's mother, I hung up and athered my thoughts. Maryam came outside and saw me itting with my head in my chest, shaken up.

"What's wrong?"

"Nothing. She's not coming."

I didn't want to explain everything to Maryam until fter the graduation and celebration. So, I just left it at that nd hoped she wouldn't ask me for details. She didn't. The ;raduation was beautiful. Maryam, her brown eyes opened vide with excitement. She wore a designer outfit, a short and ›louse set, under the graduation gown.

"Daddy, I feel like a secret agent," she meant that her outfit vasn't traditional. And that's what made her so beautiful. The vay she expressed herself. Her ability to make light of life. And 1ot get caught up with what other people thought about her.

ALTHEA JEWEL

TWENTY-ONE

The next day we went on our cruise trip that had been planned six months ago. I like fishing boats. But I don't particularly care for cruise ships. Too many people. I never thought about it. But I guess that makes me a bit of a germaphobe.

Well, I put that fear to the side because Maryam asked for the cruise. And it gave me time to reflect and think how it would feel to raise my girls. Up to now, I'd only dreamt of being a full-time dad. I thought it had to be the way it was when I was growing up. But I found out that there's always another way. It wasn't gonna be easy. I guess, just like building a house, all you need is a strong foundation.

When Jasmine's parents were ready to send my daughters home, I was ready. That evening, I turned the sprinklers on to water my front lawn as the sun was setting. I could hear my neighbor's dogs barking and the sound of a small engine plane overhead. We got the house in order. Organized the cabinets. Stocked the refrigerator. The girls were excited to be united again. Halimah jumped into my arms she started to cry. That's all it took for me to start crying. Gentle tears. Happy tears.

"Daddy what are you sad about?"

Maryam answered, "He's not sad Halimah. He's happy to see us back together."

Nee Nee, now 8, tightly holding her brown baby doll interrupted. "Is Mama coming here to live with us?"

Maryam answered decisively, "Not now."

"Oh," she said questioning her big sister's answer. "Then where am I going to sleep?" It felt like a dream. Now with no more tears.

"In your room," I said. "Follow me."

After the girls were settled, we watched television in the den before going to bed. That first night was like a beautiful dream. Up late. Eating popcorn and laughin' until it was almost midnight. Maryam tucked my youngest daughter in bed and kissed her forehead.

"Maryam."

"Uh huh."

"I love you."

"I love you too, silly." I keep a night light on in the hallway. And I've always kept my bedroom door cracked open.

"Goodnight," all three shouted out to me from down the hallway.

"Pleasant dreams." Finally, my girls were back home.

TWENTY-TWO

People are influenced by their own comfort zones. Very few of us are willing to cross any boundaries. Even when it's for the best to reach out to those involved. Our children. I decided for now, to live in the moment. Enjoy my daughters. And pray for Aaron's protection while he's still away.

Halimah knelt on a chair, leaning over the sink while Maryam washed her hair. New hair products. Maryam was becoming a hairdresser of sorts. Halimah's thick curly hair sometimes took over an hour to maintain. Twenty minutes later, the chair was placed back at the table. Maryam rinsed out the fruity fragranced shampoo and conditioner. Halimah breathed a sigh of relief while holding a towel over her head.

"What about Nee Nee?" she asked.

"Hers tomorrow, Saturday...you know that." On Sunday all of us go to the park. Then to a local restaurant. Everybody admires my beautiful girls.

"All girls?"

"One boy. But he's in California." Single dads weren't very popular in the 90's. We existed. Less so here in the south. Must've been a few locals that tried to latch on and become my wife. Old and young women. Batting eyelashes and lifting skirts to get attention.

"I can't believe a young handsome businessman like you is not married."

I nodded. "My girls are no trouble…not at all." Oh, I dated occasionally. I have a babysitter to watch the girls when I go out on the town. Sometimes after midnight if the company was really good. Sometimes platonic. A few even got physical to the point of making my toes curl. But I didn't bring anyone home.

"Curtis you need to settle down and find yourself a good wife."

"Nah Ma, I don't need that type of drama in my life."

"Sweetheart, every man needs a good woman."

"Ha, you tellin' me what I need now?" There was silence while I thought carefully…of what to say.

"Ma, I'm sorry I sounded disrespectful…but I am doing just fine…all by myself."

The next six years passed quickly. It was 2001. Maryam 23. Halimah 15. And Naomi 13. We were happy, healthy, and going strong. Jasmine was finally getting her life back together. I built that second house so she could visit and see the girls whenever she wanted to. She was surprised that she wouldn't be stayin' in the main house. Nope, I know when I've had enough. 2001 was crazy. You remember. September 11th. The World Trade Center was attacked. Aaron had just transferred out that way, New York, Columbia University.

Allison Whitfield finally called me back. She was hysterical, "Oh my God Curtis, I'm freaking out!"

"Calm down Alee," I said, rustling on my pillow trying to open my eyes. My eyes strained to focus on the clock on my nightstand…12:15am.

"How can you sleep after the bombings…should we bring him back home?"

"I told you not to send him out there in the first place."

"Damnit Curtis, you're blaming me?"

"I'm not blaming anybody…it wasn't in our control." By now, I'm in my bathroom, set the phone down on speaker while I lift the toilet seat. I didn't realize how loud going to the bathroom sounds in the middle of the night.

"Oh my God, are you peeing while I'm on the phone?"

I grumbled, "Look, I was asleep and you call in the middle of the night and I had to go." I flushed the toilet and turned on the sink and washed my hands. "What do want me to do?" I said as I picked up the phone again.

"I just want him back home."

"Look, he's not your little boy anymore. What does he want?"

"I don't know…I didn't ask him."

"Well sounds like you need to stop blowing things out of proportion and ask him." Then a loud click. No bye. No nothing else. She just hung up. Same ole same ole. The next morning was quiet. Wednesday is usually a good day. I haven't worked on Wednesday in years. It's my get the house and my thoughts in order day. While they're at school, I grocery shop and prepare a couple days of meals. Then I go jogging. The neighborhood is filling up with more houses. I love the trees. I love the North Carolina seasons. I love chilly nights and warm days. That's what initially drew me to move from California.

The girls talked me into getting a puppy. Can't say no to that. I met a few neighbors and kept my construction hat on until I was 40. Went into real estate and became a broker before my back went out doing hard labor.

Mr. Williamson across the street waved as I set my outgoing mail in the box. "How's it going Curtis?"

"Everybody's fine Darryl…you and the wife and kids?"

"Doing good Curtis, doing good."

TWENTY-THREE

In 2004, even though we hadn't spoken, Aaron Whitfield was about to graduate from NYU. I was the proudest father in America. Before I could let it all sink in, my telephone rang.

"Hello."

"Hey Curtis!" I recognized his voice, Marvin Whitfield, I almost hung up.

"Look cuz, I know you want to hang up, I can't blame you."

"What do you want Marvin?"

"I just wanted to congratulate you…Aaron, college grad, and about to go to law school!"

I'm thinkin' yes, my son's doing great, but why are you calling me, we ain't cool like that. He just kept on talking.

"'I know you supported him all these years and I just…"

I cut him off, "What happened?"

"Okay," he said, "I'll get to the point."

He went on to say, "You know, Allison got married."

"And?"

"Yea, she braggin' like he's an airline pilot, big shot businessman. She has no idea."

"Stop beatin' around the bush Marvin, just tell me."

"Her man is a hustler, a crook, an international thug."

"And I'm supposed to believe you with your history?"

"Curtis man, that was my uncle's idea..."

I shouted, "Marvin. I don't want to hear about anybody else's problems. You hear me?"

He was nervous. "Yeah, oh, Curtis...I hear you."

"I appreciate that Marvin."

I hung up. I wondered was there any truth to what he'd said Whatever happens in my ex's house is not my business.

I was proud of Aaron. Going to be a lawyer. But college isn't for everybody. Maryam stopped going after two years and now operates her own hair salon.

"Dad."

"Yes Halimah."

"Me and Nee Nee are on our way to the shop."

"Okay. You girls be careful."

I was opening my mail and noticed a letter from the car insurance company. I was surprised. It wasn't time for any renewal.

I put my reading glasses on, and took the last sip from my coffee cup.

There was a change of vehicles with an increase on the policy that I pay for Aaron's car. 2005 Range Rover, almost doubled the price. What? Alee never mentioned this to me.

"Hello."

"Hey Alee, it's Curtis, how ya doin'?"

"Fine."

"Say listen. I just got a letter from the car insurance with a change of vehicles for Aaron."

After a long "ohhh" she went on to say, "I've been so busy, I'm sorry, I forgot to call you about that."

She gives me this long, drawn out story about her husband, Robert, buying the car and shipping it to New York. And Mr. Big-baller-shot-caller is an airline pilot and he's somewhere over the Atlantic Ocean right now.

"I thought we sent him to New York to get an education?"

No comment.

Then I added, "Most of the people out there don't even drive cars...Alee what were you thinking?" I could hear some nervous tapping sound in the background. Maybe it was a pen or something.

"Curtis, don't be jealous that he just wants to do for us."

"He's my son. I've taken care of him financially since day one." The tapping sound stopped.

"I'm sorry Curtis. I didn't know you'd be so upset about it."

"Please don't change any paperwork that has my name tied to it."

"I'll get Robert to buy Aaron a separate policy."

"It sounds like you need to get Robert to get his priorities straight." I went ahead and paid the bill. But after that, I thought that maybe Alee was in over her head on this one. Maybe she did marry a crook.

I raised my daughters to be confident and forgiving Black women with strength to endure and forgiveness for everything else. My son married at 28. And when Azure, my first grandchild was born, we were finally reunited. When Aaron's wife, Tyesha called, I thought it was a prank. Then she put him on the phone and I realized it was really for real.

They invited me to their home in Northern California.

"How long has it been?" Tyesha asked me.

"Too long," I smiled, holding my granddaughter.

Aaron had done well for himself. Found a little piece of heaven in Berkeley. The baby kept her gaze on me, then yawned and fell asleep.

"You hungry dad? Want something to eat?"

I chuckled, "God you sound like me!"

"I know dad, that freaked Ty out."

Not only his voice. He was the spittin' image of a younger me. Broad shoulders. Muscular arms. Same dimple in his chin. A little taller though. I'm six feet. And he's about six-feet-two.

"Have you talked with my mom lately?"

"No son, I haven't."

"Well she's okay now...but it was sketchy for awhile."

And that's when he told me about Robert Leveaux. Died in a suspicious limo crash. Feds took the house, business, and the cars.

"I'm just grateful that you and your mother are safe. That's all that matters."

We sat side by side watchin' the clouds in the distance.

"Yea dad, see those clouds? They're moving away."

Tyesha bundled the baby tighter and rocked her gently. "Uh huh, I guess you're right son. Those clouds not comin' back this way." We laughed. Then walked together back into the house.

It took from 1982 to now, 2011, for me to start a relationship with my son.

Aaron 29. Maryam 32. Halimah 24. Naomi "Nee Nee" Morris 22.

"Ma won't you come with us to the baptism?" She pushed a gift in my hands for the baby.

"I'll meet your granddaughter soon."

I hugged my mother tight. "Okay Ma."

We drove up north in Maryam's SUV. Luckily we only made two stops. Restroom break. And a Starbuck's run. I found a cool radio station that was playin' an oldie but goodie that reminded me of my youth. Bounce, Rock, Skate and Roll. I remember showing off my moves at the skating rink with this song.

"Yeah, that's Vaughan Mason from the 80's."

The girls danced in their seats and sang right along with me. My co-pilot Maryam was paying close attention to the road. We finally eased onto Northbrae Community Church parking lot.

"We made it!"

They unbuckled their seat belts while I positioned the car mirror, then smoothed my hand over my salt-and-pepper goatee.

"Okay dad, you look good, now get moving," Halimah giggled.

First person we saw was Allison. She still looked the same. She was holding onto her new husband's arm. He looked like a decent cat.

"Hello. I'm Curtis."

We shook hands.

Several family members attended, except for Traci. No one mentioned her.

"Dad!" Aaron motioned me to sit up front with him and the baby. Me and the girls moved to the row next to him.

While Allison and her parents sat in the row behind us.

I was happy and sad, all at the same time. My girls barely knew their brother. Had missed every milestone. Every holiday. Every celebration. Then I focused on the preacher, reciting holy prayers. I smiled as he reached for the silver receptacle...poured water onto my granddaughter's head. She didn't cry.

Afterwards, we all met up in the parking lot. I looked up and saw two yellow butterflies dancing away from the crowd. It was a beautiful day.

Mr. Whitfield walked towards me. His hand was unsteady. He stopped and leaned a little on his walking stick. The expression on his face was not as I remembered. His eyes had softened. Everyone else, still gathered around the baby. They weren't worried about us. He said, "I've made some mistakes over my lifetime."

I listened.

He continued, "And I want you to know...Curtis, I truly regret mistreating you the way I did." It was so unexpected. And while he kept talkin' I imagined myself as a young kid. Outta high school. Lovesick over his daughter. I could feel the sun on my face, with my scooter turned sideways on the concrete between us. And I wanted to embrace the impossible possibility of him...leaning down...extending his hand towards me. The sunlight was shifting. He was winding up his apology. I don't know what he was saying. I just knew I didn't need him to help me stand back on my feet.

"Yeah Curtis, like I said..."

Right then I walked closer to him and placed my hand on his shoulder and I shook him gently to get his attention.

We both made our peace.

I reassured him.

"I understand Mr. Whitfield. Everybody makes mistakes."

Made in the USA
Las Vegas, NV
01 February 2024

85193112R00135